MW01118066

A MYSTERY AT THE INN

A Mystery at The Inn

JOHN VASZKO

11-08-08

YELLOWBACK MYSTERIES
JAMES A. ROCK & COMPANY, PUBLISHERS
ROCKVILLE • MARYLAND

A Mystery at the Inn by John Vaszko

is an imprint of JAMES A. ROCK & CO., PUBLISHERS

Author's Note: *There is an inn in Somerset, Pennsylvania. It is called "The Inn at Georgian Place" and is listed on the National Registry of Historical Places. The building is used as a backdrop for the story however, the story is fictional. In most instances actual names and descriptive details have been altered to protect the identities of the characters. Information regarding the historical aspects of the building and the owner were researched through The Pennsylvania Historical Society located in Somerset, Pennsylvania.*

Address comments and inquiries to:
YELLOWBACK MYSTERIES
James A. Rock & Company, Publishers
9710 Traville Gateway Drive, #305
Rockville, MD 20850
E-mail:
jrock@rockpublishing.com lrock@rockpublishing.com
Internet URL: www.rockpublishing.com

Paperback ISBN-13/EAN: 978-1-59663-656-9
Hardback ISBN-13/EAN: 978-1-59663-721-4

Library of Congress Control Number: 2007941746

Printed in the United States of America

First Edition: 2008

For Susan

the reason all this was possible

ACKNOWLEDGMENTS

My heartfelt thanks go out to Jon and the staff, both past and present, for their caring and dedication in making the Inn our home away from home. I also want to thank the residents of Somerset, too many to mention individually, for making our visits to the Inn such memorable experiences. Their knowledge of the Zimmerman home and family have helped this story come to life. To single out any one would diminish from those I might have forgotten to mention.

Special thanks are also due to family, friends and the many guests Susan and I have met and celebrated with at the Inn.

Last but surely not least, I thank the Zimmerman family for building such a marvelous home.

The Inn

As you crest the knoll and I come into view,
a placid tranquility comes over you.
My majestic frame set high on the hill,
lures you to access its calm, so tranquil.

My warmth can be felt as you enter the door,
embracing you into my stately grandeur.
The innkeeper Jon will greet with a smile,
inviting each one to stay for a while.

Thanks is to be given to the warmth of the staff,
for their love of life will make you laugh.
Enjoy your stay it will feel like home,
Its charm spreads a feeling and you'll not want to roam.

The ghosts that reside here are kind for the most,
just make sure not to anger them or your host.
Come often come soon far away from the din,
I'm here for your pleasure.

I'm the Somerset Inn.

—John Vaszko

CHAPTER ONE

"I don't know about you two but I can't wait to get away from here," said Sam as they packed up their tools and left Johnstown.

"Why are you in such a hurry to leave? Our business has had the best year ever. I, for one, would like to stay around and bask in the knowledge that this company is in the black for the second year in a row," Mike said as he put his mud caked boots up on the dashboard of their old truck.

"I'm with Sam. We have worked our asses off to wrap everything up so we can get out of here for a few weeks. The three construction sites are shut down until the weather breaks and the four houses we completed for Christmas occupancy were finished on time. We need a break and I, for one, can't wait to get to the warm sunny tropics in Cancun," said Bob.

The three had made it through the fifth year with their construction business. The Three Studs Construction Company was a dream of theirs since graduating from high school. They had spent countless summers working for their father who started a well drilling business after finding out he was on the verge of black lung disease. He managed to take his savings from working in the coal mines, and his knowledge acquired from drilling in the mines into drilling for water for the thirsty people in Somerset, Pennsylvania. His three kids helped him every summer. Sam, Mike, and Bob would assist him at new homes sites. They all lugged pipes and worked the drilling rig. None of them ever wanted to follow in their fathers footsteps of working in the coal mine or, for that matter, drilling for water. They wanted something more out of life. The three of them would watch carpenters, bricklayers, and plumbers doing their jobs on the new homes being built. All three thought it would be a lot more fun, and more lucrative, to build houses than drill for water. After a few summers helping drill for water they were sick of the drilling business. They each decided to get into the construction programs offered at their high school. If they still liked the construction business after they completed the courses, they would pool their money and find a way to start their own business.

It didn't take long to find out each of them loved the construction business. Sam enjoyed the finish carpentry. Mike was a natural bricklayer, and Bob loved plumbing and electrical work. When they told their father their goal of starting their own business, they were juniors in high school. He couldn't have been happier for them. He wanted them to be anything but coal miners. He knew Mike and Bob were big strapping men and would be able to take the rigors of the construction business, but he wasn't sure about Sam. Sam was a sickly kid growing up and spent a lot of time in doctor's offices. By the time Sam became a teenager the health problems seemed to subside, but Sam never seemed to have the strength to be in the construction business. Sam's tenacity proved a match for Mike's and Bob's physical strength. As a finish carpenter Sam's craftsmanship was amazing. The cabinets and staircases made in high school shop class were as good, if not better than any made in the county by seasoned professionals. Sam was offered jobs with every construction company that saw the skill level and quality workmanship produced. There was no reason to believe Sam wouldn't be a successful carpenter.

"I wish dad were still alive. He would have loved to go on vacation with us," said Sam.

"Dad would never have taken a vacation. He never took a day off from the well drilling business, or his days in the coal mines. What makes you think he would go on a vacation with us?" asked Bob.

"You're right, but it was a nice thought, the four of us drinking Tequila in Cancun," said Sam.

"He would have been saying you three won't make any money throwing it away on a vacation," said Mike.

"Well he's gone now. He finally made it to be with Mom. He talked about seeing her in heaven for the past ten years. I hope he got his wish," said Bob.

"Okay that's enough of this depressing talk. Dad has been gone for six months and we are leaving tomorrow morning. You two packed?" asked Sam.

"You've got to be kidding. I don't even know where my suitcase is," said Mike.

"When I drop you off you better get your asses in gear. The plane leaves from Pittsburgh at 8:30 a.m. sharp. We have to be there two hours before flight time. I'll pick you up at 5 a.m." said Sam.

The phone rang and interrupted Sam. "Three Studs Construction Company, Sam speaking. Oh, hi Jon. How's everything at the Inn? You want us to bid on a job for you? What do you have in mind?" Sam listened to Jon for a few minutes. "Better yet, how about I come over in about two hours. I have to drop off an estimate in Boswell and should be back in a couple of hours? We can talk over a drink at your new bar," said Sam and hung up the phone.

"That sounded like Jon at the Inn. What does he want?" asked Bob.

"He is interested in some renovations. It should be mostly inside work. It could be what we need after we get back from our vacation. I'm going to stop by and see exactly what he wants. I'll tell you about it when I see you two tomorrow morning,"

Sam exclaimed to Bob and Mike, “I can’t wait to hang this coat up and only have to wear a tee shirt for two glorious weeks on the beach.”

CHAPTER TWO

"It's nice to see the sun again," Andrew said to Raul as he piled his shovels into the pick-up truck.

"The sun is most welcomed after all that rain," Raul replied.

The two men had been working together for the past two years at an archaeological dig at Cape Catoche, a small town nearly twenty miles north of Cancun, Mexico. The dig was in an area Andrew believed, from his studies, was a location for a large Mayan city. The area consisted of a large limestone plateau on the coast of the Gulf of Mexico. The location was presumed to be sacred to the ancient Mayans. Andrew was sure a city had been built within the natural limestone caves. The Mayan civilization had experienced ship builders that would make the area a perfect place to construct a city.

"That last hurricane was the biggest one yet," said Andrew.

"We must be making the Mayan gods very angry with our digging and exploring of their sacred area. This has been the third major hurricane this month," Raul said to Andrew as he added more equipment to the back of the truck.

"I heard on the news that we have had more rain this season than any on record. Maybe you are right about angering the Mayan gods. Do you want me to call off the dig?" asked Andrew mostly in jest.

"No, *señor* my people need the money and there are wondrous things to be found when we find the old city," Raul replied completing the loading of the truck.

Andrew had received a grant from an anonymous donor to the Penn State University Archaeological Department. The money was to be used to search for a presumed lost Mayan city on the Yucatan Peninsula. Andrew was pretty sure the money was from his father. Andrew's father owned a large steel mill that he built up from nothing. It was now the largest independently owned steel mill in the country. Andrew's father wanted him to join the family and become a partner in the mill but he was never interested in the steel business. He left that to his two younger brothers. He was happy doing what he did, and he knew his father was sad that he didn't want to join the rest of the family, but he was extremely proud of him for striking out on his own. Andrew was always an independent person. Often when his father would get upset with him he would say, "You are too much like me when I was growing up. I guess the old adage of having a son just like you has come to fruition in this family. If only your mother were alive to see how you have grown into your own person she would have been proud."

Andrew worked three jobs to pay for his college education. He had the same gene pool as his father and wanted only to succeed from the toil of his own hands.

Since the donation to the college was anonymous, he couldn't be sure it was from his father, so he accepted it. He was now in his last month of the grant. He had found quite a number of artifacts over the past twenty-three months but he had far too little to show for it. The valuable pieces had been confiscated by the local police department.

The local police were more than policemen. They were also the local military. They were the judge and jury on any legal matter that fell in their jurisdiction. They were, to put it bluntly, crooks. In the political arena, they were corrupt. Anything of value was taken as a treasure of the country of Mexico and supposedly shipped to the state museum in Mexico City. Andrew was getting tired of these corrupt officials taking everything of significance he found. Many times he wished he had some of the old objects he had found to compare them to new inscriptions he unearthed. He wanted to be able to analyze some of the items he had found through carbon dating. When he asked where he could go to examine the items they took, the police would just say they were safe in the museum and couldn't be seen. Andrew wanted to find out if the items these local police took ever got to the Mexico City Museum. To satisfy his curiosity to the corruptness of the local police, he planted a Global Positioning System micro chip in one of the urns that was to be taken by the police to the Museum. He followed the trail of the urn with his GPS tracking system to a wealthy man's house in the suburbs of Mexico City. Andrew sat in his truck. He used his computer to find out the name of the man who lived in the house. The man's name was Miguel Hernandos.

Andrew sat in the truck as the rain started pelting the windshield of the truck. He became very angry when he realized all of his hard work was being sold to someone who probably had no idea of the historical value the antiquities possessed. He couldn't take the fact that all his work had been stolen from him and sold to this Miguel Hernandos. He got out of his truck and stood outside the gated mansion and seethed. The house was a bastion, probably filled with hundreds of antiquities of the Mayans stolen from him and other hard working Archeologists. They were bought and paid for and were never destined to see the inside of a museum.

It was now pouring down rain. Andrew stood in front of the large house where his urn had been taken. Andrew, wearing a large brimmed hat and poncho, stood outside the walled home looking through the Iron Gate that led to the main entrance. The rain was pouring off his hat in rivulets. He was losing control by the minute. The longer he stood thinking about all the hours of study and digging, the more he lost control of his temper. He wasn't a man to get angry often, but when he did, all his friends knew it was best to stay far away from him. This time his anger was directed at whoever lived in the big house. The man inside had enough money and political clout to steal treasures that belonged to the country. They should not be coveted by one man. He pushed the button on the call box next to the Iron Gate.

"May I help you?" a female voice answered in Spanish.

"I would like to talk with the owner Mister Hernandos please," Andrew replied in Spanish through clenched teeth.

"Who are you please?" asked the voice.

Andrew told her, "I am the Archeologist whose discoveries have been stolen by the man who lives in this house."

"One moment please," she said.

In a minute she came back on the intercom, "I am sorry there is no one here that wishes to talk with you," the voice said and the speaker went dead.

As she finished speaking, the giant front doors of the house opened. Two men in clear plastic raincoats came out of the house brandishing shotguns carried under their raincoats. They looked out to the gate where Andrew stood. Andrew became more furious. He had a hard time controlling himself. His fists were knotted around the bars of the gate and his knuckles were snow white. The two men slowly walked toward him with their shotguns held casually in the crooks of their arms. Andrew stood watching the two men get closer and closer. The taller of the two yelled at Andrew in Spanish.

"Gringo move away from the gate. Move on. Move on."

Andrew didn't move a step. His hands were clamped around the bars of the gate. The men came up to the gate and shouted at him again.

"Get away from here before we move you away."

Andrew didn't move. He just stared at the taller of the two men as rain cascaded off the front of his hat. The shorter of the two men took his shotgun and smashed the butt of the gun against Andrew's gate wrapped fingers. Andrew heard the finger crack before he felt the searing pain. He let go of the bar but continued to stare at the taller of the two men.

"I will see you again," Andrew said as he backed up, turned and walked away.

"Strange man," the tall man said to his partner.

"I broke at least one of his fingers and he didn't even make a sound. I hope I don't ever meet him again," the shorter of the two said.

"I'm afraid you will. The next time you better do more than break his fingers if you expect to live through the experience. Now let's get out of this damnable rain."

CHAPTER THREE

"Jon, it's good to see you. I haven't been here for a while. How is everything going?"

"Things are doing pretty well. I like your coat. I need one like that," said Jon as he greeted Sam in the foyer.

Looking at the ten foot tall Ionic columns Sam removed the parka and said, "Every time I come in here, I hope I will have a chance to build something like this before my construction career is over."

"Don't forget this place was built in 1915 at a cost of over $300,000. Today it would cost millions to build."

Sam was well aware that the house was unique in its day. Daniel Zimmerman, the original owner, was at that time the richest man in the county and could afford to build it.

Sam had written a paper on Daniel Zimmerman in High School and could recall many of the facts uncovered during the research. Daniel started his climb to fortune when, at the ripe old age of fourteen, he left home to raise cattle in North Dakota. Apparently he read an article in a farming magazine stating that the grass in the Dakota's was so rich in nutritional value that cattle could be raised and brought to market fatter and sooner. From that beginning Daniel became the largest privately owned cattleman in the country. He had accumulated hundreds of thousands of acres from the Dakota's to California and regularly shipped over 40,000 head of cattle to markets each year.

Being an astute businessman he then went into coal mining and owned more than 140,000 acres of coal fields in the Somerset area. By the age of forty-five he became the largest independent coal operator in the county. His association with the other rich coal operators, namely the Berwind family, was his connection to Horace Trumbauer. Horace had designed and built a mansion for the Berwin family in Newport, Rhode Island.

The architect, Mister Horace Trumbauer designed many homes for the rich and famous in the early 1900's. This was one of the smallest homes Trumbauer designed. Sam was hoping some day to get a chance to see some of Trumbauer's larger homes in Newport, Rhode Island.

Sam recalled that Daniel had owned the land which the Inn now stands on for a long time. The parcel consisted of a parcel of over forty acres. He started at least ten years prior to the construction of the house to landscape the property. Hundreds of fruit trees, as well as, shrubbery and flowers were planted before the plans for the house were complete.

Sam came back to reality as Jon said, "… and there isn't anyone in the county today who could afford to build like this."

"I remember, Jon. I have been a life-long resident of Somerset, just like you. Remember we lived near each other on the other side of town. Now let's get a beer from your new bar and you can tell me what the Three Studs Construction Company can do for you. Before you tell me you want something done by tomorrow, we are going to be closed after today for the next two weeks."

"Are you three going on vacation together again?" asked Jon with a laugh in his voice.

"We are and this time we are going to Cancun," Sam said.

"I know it's not going to be Aruba again. Haven't the three of you been told not to go back to the island?" asked Jon laughingly.

"It wasn't like that. We were minding our own business when these two guys came running down the beach. The first guy yells to us to stop the guy that was chasing him. We thought we were doing our 'Good Samaritan' deed for the day and stopped the second guy. We didn't know the first guy was the robber. We stopped a policeman who was chasing him. We didn't get thrown off the island, but we did make the newspapers. It was an honest mistake."

"As I remember, the three of you were drinking heavily that day, according to the newspaper article, and were kept in jail overnight," said Jon laughing again.

"Okay so everyone in Somerset knew what happened by the time we got back. It wasn't all bad. We ended up getting a lot of free publicity for our business."

"I've always wanted to ask you, who came up with the name The Three Stud's Construction Company anyway?" asked Jon as they sat at the newly finished bar.

"I guess I did. It's kind of catchy isn't it?"

"Yes, but let's get to business. I know you want to get out of here and get ready for your trip and I have twenty-five people coming for dinner tonight. Here is what I am thinking I want to do."

Jon told Sam of his remodeling ideas. Sam took notes and did a little measuring.

"I'll talk it over with my brothers on our way down on the plane tomorrow and I'll get back to you in a day or two. I'll fax you our proposal. Thanks for the chance to bid on the job, and thanks for the beer. The bar looks beautiful. See you in two weeks. Stay warm," Sam said closing the inner doors to the vestibule.

CHAPTER FOUR

The dig site was a half mile from their camp. The men would meet Andrew and Raul just after the sun came up every day, except Sunday. The six of them would ride in the truck to the dig site. They hadn't been to the site for the last three days due to the hurricane that made a direct hit on the area. Every time the men went back to the dig site after a major rain, the topography of the land would look different.

Limestone would dissolve from the rainwater passing through the soil, picking up acids from the dirt. The dissolved limestone would wash away and new openings would appear in the rocks. Over time, the dissolved limestone could form caves or sink holes might appear when the roof of a cave collapsed from the weight of the wet dirt above. Over the centuries, caves and sink holes had honeycombed the area.

The Mayans had started living in the area over 3,000 years ago. If Andrew could see differences in the topography over the short period of time he was at the site, *think what the area was like when the Mayans were living there,* he thought to himself. Andrew got excited each and every day he drove to the site. This could be the day he finds the entrance to the lost city. He would be famous and he would be able to have a larger dig force and more time could be spent at the dig site. He may be able to rid himself of the police that stole his findings. Yes, this could be the day, he thought to himself.

"How are your fingers? Are you going to be able to help us dig today?" asked Raul.

"I will remember those two men and their boss with every ounce of dirt I move," said Andrew as he tried to flex his bandaged fingers.

CHAPTER FIVE

It was cold, very cold, and dark as Sam and Bob pulled up to Mike's home. Mike lived in the old homestead. The three of them had inherited the place after their father died. Sam already was living in a new doublewide trailer and Bob was renting a farm. Bob enjoyed taking care of animals and being out of town. Sam liked the newness of the trailer and the compactness of trailer life. Mike lived with Dad until Dad's heart and lungs gave out. He took care of him and he kept up the repairs on the place. When Dad died and the will was read, Sam and Bob had already decided that Mike would get title to the place. Mike protested and wanted to pay them back for their rightful share. Sam and Bob convinced him he more than paid his share by taking care of Dad over the last few years. Mike's house was the one located nearest the entrance to the interstate. It was now 5:25 a.m. Sam and Bob were waiting for Mike to make his appearance

"Get in the car. We're running late," yelled Sam through the partially rolled down car window as Mike appeared in the open doorway.

Mike came out and hurriedly locked the door.

"What is that thing you are carrying?" asked Bob.

"That's my suitcase."

"Ben Franklin had a newer suitcase than that. Where did you find that thing?" asked Sam.

"It's Dad's old one. It was up in the attic. I can't find mine," Mike said as he jumped in the back seat with his suitcase.

"Let's go Sam. We don't want to be late for the flight. There's a bar in Cancun waiting for us," said Bob.

"And there's a beach with the hot sun beating down on it ready for my body," Sam said as they drove to the interstate highway for their trip to the Pittsburgh Airport.

CHAPTER SIX

"You broke his fingers?" asked Miguel in Spanish.

"I heard the bones break when I hit them with the butt of the shotgun," responded the little man.

"I hope the broken fingers don't stop him from getting me new items from the Mayans," Miguel said between his fits of laughter.

The three men stood in the foyer of the mansion and laughed.

Miguel only stopped laughing when his cell phone started ringing. He shooed the two men away.

"Yes," Miguel said as he walked onto the marble patio at the rear of the house.

"Sir this is Captain Sanchez. I was told our digger is on his way to your home. I just found out he was doing this. I hope he doesn't cause you any trouble. I didn't know or I would have stopped him," the captain said apologetically.

"He was here and we took care of him. He may not be able to dig much for the next few days, but other than a few broken fingers he is alright," Miguel said as he sat down by the pool.

"I'm sorry for the trouble. It won't happen again. I will shoot him if I have to. He won't bother you. I promise," the captain said.

"Captain Sanchez it has been handled. I know you have everything under control. All I ask is that you continue to come to me first when you have something to sell. My cousin the Magistrate agrees with what you are doing. I have also talked with the General and he is pleased with your handling of the situation. As long as we are notified first, there will not be a problem. It is important that you send some of the items to the Museum to make sure they don't get wise to what you are doing. You know it isn't in our best interest if you are caught with treasures that rightfully belong to the country of Mexico. We will help you all we can but there are things even we cannot control. Do I make myself clear?" asked Miguel as he sat looking over his 3,000 acre estate. Sipping steaming sweet coffee from a china cup, he waited for an answer.

"I understand," said Sanchez.

Sanchez hung up the phone only after he heard the click of Miguel's phone.

Captain Sanchez would now have to go home to change his shirt. The conversation with Miguel had made him sweat uncontrollably. His sweating has been a problem all his life. Whenever he got into a tense situation he would start to sweat uncontrollably. He hated his problem but he hated more the idea of going back home during the day. His wife Maria would be cleaning the house or nursing their fifth child. Although he loved her with all his heart, she was starting to look like a cow with her udder always out feeding a child. He missed the trim figure she had when they were first married. Why did she want to have so many children? She seemed happy to have a new child each year of their marriage.

It was getting tougher and tougher each year to feed and cloth all of them. If he didn't have his little scheme of taking everything the archeologist found and selling the best pieces to Miguel, he would be a very poor man. He needed to make sure he didn't let any of the finds from the dig slip through his fingers. He had pulled his two cousins into the deal of stealing the treasure. He needed their help to watch the men at the dig every day. He couldn't do it alone and it was always good to have someone else to blame in case the officials from Mexico City ever came to check on what was happening in his area. He knew Miguel had a lot of pull, but if high government officials became involved, he would be left out by himself to take the punishment. He had learned from Miguel. He now had others to blame. He didn't want to have any of his relatives in jail but it was better that they go to jail than him.

Maybe he had left a shirt over at Carlota's. It would be better to go there than home. Thinking of Carlota brought a smile to his face. She was a young girl who would do anything for him. She had shared her bed with him for the past six months. She was trim and her young skin was a delight to touch. The only problem was he would have to spend a few hours with her. She always wanted to get him in bed. It was nice to have such a beautiful young lady around, but today he had to keep his eye on the American archeologist. He didn't have time to spend the day in bed. During the days of the hurricane, he could take a few hours in the afternoon to play with his Carlota, but now that the men would be back at the dig site he needed to keep an eye on them. He didn't have the time to play with Carlota. He would just have to take a new shirt from the supply closet. It was worth the cost of having to buy the shirt from the government so he could get back to his job. He was Captain of the police force and he did have to look good on the job.

CHAPTER SEVEN

"That was close," said Mike as they sat in their seats on the plane.

"Where did all those people come from?" asked Sam.

"We were lucky to find a parking space, but we're here now. Let's get a drink and enjoy the ride," said Bob.

It's only 8:30 in the morning. There will be plenty of time to drink when we are on the beach sunning ourselves," Sam said.

"Where are we staying?" asked Bob.

"You know, you have it made. You sit in the car on the way to the airport, you sit at the airport while we take care of the tickets, you are sitting on your ass in this plane, and now you become interested in where we are staying. Why don't you get involved in the planning?" asked Sam.

"Too many cooks spoil the soup," said Bob.

"It's too many cooks spoil the broth, not soup. We are staying at the Empress Hotel. It's right on the beach. It has bar service on the beach; wind surfing, snorkeling, volley ball, and three bars. If you want to eat, there are four restaurants in the hotel and plenty of other places to eat and drink within walking distance. Any other questions your majesty?" asked Sam.

"Do we have separate rooms or are we all going to bunk together?" Bob asked.

"After all the bitching last year, we have separate rooms."

"It wasn't bad last year. I slept like a baby."

"You did, but Mike couldn't get a wink of sleep with all of your snoring. He refused to be in the same room with you again."

"Well, that little pansy. I never complained about his farting all night," Bob said.

Mike leaned over from his seat on the other side of Sam and said, "How would you know. You fell asleep as soon as your head hit the pillow."

"But I did have to get up in the middle of the night to take a pee. Man, it was bad. I'm surprised the maid didn't charge you double to come into the room in the morning."

"Okay, that's enough, Mister Fart and Mister Snore. Give the other people on this plane a break. You sound like a pair of kids. Let's talk about the job Jon wants us to do at the Inn. Jon wants some modifications. The new bar is doing well and he wants to make some additional improvements. He wants to add another room on the third floor and a few repairs in the basement. I told him I would get back to him as soon as I could. It would make a good project for us until we can get to the other job sites in the spring." Sam said, picking up a notebook and showing them a few sketches of what Jon wanted.

The three of them spent the rest of the flight working out the best approach to accomplish what Jon wanted at The Inn. The flight landed as they completed the cost estimate for the job.

The three had gotten to the hotel without a hitch and didn't waste any time hitting the beach. After a few hours in the sun, they asked about the best places to eat and drink. "Isn't this great?" exclaimed Bob as he sat on the beach with a beer in his hand.

"It doesn't get any better than this," said Sam.

"Hey, there is a man running down the beach. Should we stop him? He may be a crook." said Mike laughing.

CHAPTER EIGHT

"Captain Sanchez, the archaeologists and his men are getting ready to go back to the dig site," said Sanchez's cousin over the two-way radio.

"Well, follow them and don't let them see you."

"What do I do if they see me?"

"Stay with them. Watch every move. We must make sure the Archeologist doesn't try to steal any of our country's treasures," Sanchez said hanging up the two-way radio.

Sanchez buttoned up the clean, dry shirt and decided it was time for lunch. After he ate, he would see to the other duties he had as the police chief of Cape Catoche. He would have to trust his men to watch the dig site.

CHAPTER NINE

Andrew finally reached the dig site. The trip had been more difficult than normal. The dirt road was full of puddles of water and where there wasn't standing water, there was mud. The trip took twice the regular time. Andrew continued to think about how he was going to get even with that rich bastard who was taking all the treasures he had found. His ideas of getting even became more graphic in his mind every time his aching fingers shot pain to his brain. There wasn't a doctor for miles. He did the best he could setting his own broken fingers. The only competent doctors were in Cancun. He would go there after the day's work. The swelling wasn't as bad as he had expected. The breaks must be clean. The skin wasn't broken, which helped his worrying about the chance of infection. Every time the fingers started to ache (which was most of the time) he thought of ways to get back at the two men and their boss, Miguel Hernandos. He would find some way to get back at them. He couldn't forget the biggest pain in the ass of all, Captain Sanchez.

They finally arrived at the dig site. The areas where they had been digging were full of water. It was going to take a few hours to get the water scooped out of the trenches before they could continue with their work. Andrew decided to let the others remove the water. He wanted to explore the surrounding area to see what the storm may have uncovered. The men grabbed their shovels and pails and headed to the trenches to remove the accumulated water.

"When you get the water out of the ditch call me I'll be over that hill looking around," said Andrew pointing toward a mound a few hundred yards away.

The ground was mushy as he walked. He had learned, over the past two years walking the site, that the ground in this area could be very unstable. He had fallen through sink holes a few times but luckily had not hurt himself. The sink holes were only a few feet deep, and the ground was so soft his landing was more embarrassing than damaging. All he had ever gotten was a wet ass.

Today was different. The storm had dumped more water than all the other storms he had been through combined. With each step the ground squished under his feet. For some reason he became more excited about the possibilities of something big being uncovered. As Andrew crested the hill he could see a crater directly in front of him. He cautiously walked around the sink hole. He was half-way around the depression when the ground gave way under him. He didn't just fall a few feet this time. He went down at least ten feet. It was like riding an elevator without brakes. When he stopped falling, he was still standing upright, but he was now facing the wall of a cave. He stood for a minute to let the mud and grass settle, and to let his eyes get used to the partial darkness. After standing a minute, he realized he had fallen into an old Mayan ruin. *Maybe this could be part of the lost city he had been looking for*, he thought.

The bright sunlight came through the opening created by his fall. It helped him see that there were picture writings on the walls. The writings were in bright reds and shades of blues. He soon realized it wasn't just a cave with writings. He had fallen through the roof of a Mayan building. The building must have been a temple because the picture writings showed many of the gods the Mayans worshiped.

Andrew wouldn't let his excitement get the better of him. He was an archaeologist first and had to make sure he didn't miss anything. As he stood in the same spot where he landed, he let his eyes further adjust to the light coming into the area. Directly in front of him were the picture graphs in the typical style of the Mayans. Each picture depicted an event they wanted to remember. The pictures depicted the Corn God showing a plentiful harvest. There were pictures that depicted the Mayans conquering the local people, including their local gods.

It was a common practice with the Mayans to include the gods of the people they conquered to be added to their worship ceremonies. It seemed to appease the people they conquered. Other pictures depicted events that happened throughout the history of the Mayans. By the time the Mayans had moved to the Yucatan, they had over 2,000 years of their dynasty recorded in picture graphs. They started in the low lands of Guatemala which archeologists called the Pre-classic Period. They then built their first pyramids around 800 BC.

The Classic Period, between A.D. 250 and A.D.900 produced fine pottery, jewelry, and large cities with carved stone statues over fifty feet tall. The Mayans developed into mathematicians and astronomers during this period. The Mayans had a number system that used a base twenty and they were the first to use the zero in their number system. They had a calendar with 365 days and believed there were five days each year that were extremely unlucky. On these five days they fasted and made human sacrifices to their gods. The picture graphs Andrew was examining reflected all these phases of Mayan life.

Andrew couldn't believe what he had literally fallen into. The room seemed to be a history of the Mayan civilization. *Maybe it was a form of Mayan library,* he thought. He would have to move further into the room to understand the depth of his find. His heart was beating out of his chest. He carefully reached into his jacket for his flashlight. Turning it on, he saw he was in a room approximately 15 feet by 15 feet. There were picture graphs carved into stone monoliths around the room. In the center of the room was a stone bench. There were stalactites hanging from the seat that reached to the floor. The light glimmered off the damp floor. Andrew realized that over the years, limestone from above had dripped down on the bench and created cave-like features on the man-made bench. Andrew walked a few steps into the room. He was careful to make sure he didn't find another sinkhole and fall further into the Mayan building. The next fall could swallow him up forever.

As he made his way toward an opening in the room, the flashlight produced enough light for him to read some of the other picture graphs. Andrew stopped at one of the monoliths. Pictures depicted the city of Chichen Itza. This city existed between 900 and 1200 A.D. and was located ten miles inland. These people must have moved from Chichen Itza to get access to the sea. The Mayans became rulers of the trade routes on land and then stretched to the sea routes. This city must have been built to help them secure some of those sea passages. Andrew moved to the last monolith before the opening into another room. This one depicted the Mayans capturing small fishing vessels. Further down the column Mayan ships seemed to be attacking larger ships that resembled Spanish Galleons. Andrew was amazed with the picture graphs. He knew the Spanish conquered the Mayans in the 1500's but there were no records that the Mayans attacked the Spanish ships. This in itself was a find that would make him a famous archeologist. He needed to see what could be found in the next room. Andrew looked at his watch. He had been gone from the dig site for only forty-five minutes. They wouldn't miss him for another hour. He had to press on. He always carried spare batteries so he wasn't worried about getting caught in the dark. The light coming in from the hole he made in the roof would help him find his way back. There was the little problem of climbing out of the room, but he would worry about that later.

Walking through the doorway Andrew started down a long hallway. The walls were hewn from the solid limestone of the cave. Stalactites from the ceiling and stalagmites forming from the floor were scattered down the length of the room. The oozing limestone made the walk slippery. The hallway was about five feet wide so Andrew could hold on and keep himself from falling. The ceiling was almost seven feet high, which was unusual for people who were only five feet tall. The only time high hallways were built was for the most sacred places. The Mayans thought the high ceilings allowed the spirits room to move around.

Andrew walked down the twenty foot hallway slipping only once. This floor had not been walked on by anyone for over a thousand years and Andrew was sure he was the only European ever to be there. His heart was racing with excitement. At the end of the hallway he came into another room. The walls reflected the light from the flashlight in an almost blinding way. The beam of the flashlight reflected off the walls in a thousand directions. Andrew wasn't sure what made the light so intense. He then realized the walls were all covered in gold. The gold still had a high polish after all the years buried in the cave. Andrew touched the walls and saw they were picture graphs inlayed in gold. The picture graphs seemed to depict a history of the city and of the king that ruled it. There were ships and strange looking god-like characters. The gold seemed to be as shiny as the day it was put on the walls. In the middle of the room was a small stone coffin sitting on a raised stone pedestal. On the top of the coffin were picture graphs showing what looked like the sun, moon, and the stars. Andrew had not seen anything like these in all the research he had done of the Mayans. Maybe the people who lived here before the Mayans worshiped the sun, moon, and stars and the Mayans incorporated those deities into their religion. The coffin was no more than three feet long. The stone box was about two feet wide. *Whoever was buried in the coffin must be a child,* Andrew thought.

As Andrew stood in the room looking at the treasure he had

found, he thought of that bastard Miguel and his lackey Captain Sanchez. He knew that all this would be in their hands. With the value of the items in this room, he wouldn't be surprised if Sanchez and Hernando didn't get him buried inside this tomb to keep him from telling anyone. His broken fingers started to ache. He had forgotten about his hand for the last hour. Now the pain was back. He had to find some way to get the knowledge of this find out of Mexico and to his colleagues back in the States. Andrew kept looking at the small coffin. He wanted to know what was inside. If he were at a dig site that wasn't watched by crooks, like Miguel and Sanchez, he would remove the coffin before anyone thought about opening it and send it for x-rays and laboratory study. In this situation all he could do was try to get the box open and see what was inside. Maybe there would be some way he could get information about the find out to others in his field. He looked at the stone top. The seal between the top and the base seemed pretty tight. He tried pushing the lid sideways, but to no avail. He needed something to pry it up. He dug into his jacket pocket for his penknife. The knife was old. His father had given it to him many years ago. He hoped it was strong enough to do what needed to be done. Andrew took the knife and ran it along the crack between the top and bottom of the box. He wanted to clear away any dirt that had accumulated over the past 1,000 years. As he slid the pen knife along the top of the box, he heard a click. The top of the coffin popped up about an inch. He slid his fingers in and pulled the top sideways. The top moved with almost no effort. The lid now was at a right angle to the bottom of the box. *That's strange,* Andrew thought. The lid must be on some kind of pivot. He would love to have the time to study how they managed to build a stone slab that moved so easily. He aimed his flashlight into the exposed top of the coffin He was treated to the sight of a body wrapped in what looked like linen cloth. It had never been reported that the Mayans mummified their dead, but here was an intact mummy of what looked like a boy king. Around the mummy's neck was a large medallion attached to a necklace. The necklace chain was thick and looked to be made of pure gold. The medallion was at least six inches in diameter. The flashlight beam hit a large red stone attached to the necklace. Next to the red stone was a green stone both stones were about the size of quail's eggs. The rest of the medallion was inlaid with clear white stones that looked to be ten, ten carat diamonds. Andrew looked closer at the two big stones. He was sure one was a ruby and the other an emerald, but the size of the stones were huge. He knew that emeralds were found in the country of Columbia but this stone was larger than any he had ever seen. The emerald had to be close to two inches in diameter, and the ruby was the same size. The stones were set in the solid gold medallion on gold prongs. Andrew picked up the medallion. It was heavy. He knew the necklace was probably worth millions of dollars to the crooks, and priceless for its historic value. If Sanchez got his hands on it he would never have the opportunity to get to see it in a museum. He knew he didn't want this treasure to get into the hands of Miguel and Sanchez. If he took this treasure back to his camp, the police would see what he found. He was tired of having everything he found taken from him and sold to people like Miguel Hernandos. He knew he couldn't get the total medallion past the police. He had to do something else. He decided he was going to try to get the stones out of the country. The first thing he needed to do was to get the necklace out of this place and hide it. Then he would need to find a way to get the stones out of the country, but that was the next step. He first would have to worry about keeping the stones out of the hands of the crooks.

Andrew had to use both hands to get the necklace off the mummy. He placed the flashlight on top of the mummy's chest. He reached under and around the neck of the mummy to feel for a clasp on the chain. There was no clasp. The chain was solid. He started to slide the chain up the mummy's back and off of the neck. As he slid the chain, something was making the chain stick.

He gave the necklace a little tug. The chain came lose, but all of a sudden, the top of the coffin started to move back to its closed position. Andrew was caught with an instant decision to make, did he grab the flashlight or the necklace. He realized he wasn't going to have time to do both. Andrew pulled the necklace clear as the coffin lid turned and slammed shut. He was now standing in the tomb with the necklace in his hand in total darkness.

His first thought was the room was going to be like something out of an *Indiana Jones* movie and slowly start to settle into the ocean drowning him, or spears were gong to come up through the floor. He didn't have a magic whip to get him out of trouble. He was standing there in total darkness, thinking he was glad he had taken an archeology class with Doctor Heilman. With the priceless necklace in his hand, he remembered the class Doctor Heilman taught during his junior year at Penn State. That summer the class went on a field trip to Egypt to study the ancient ruins at Gaza. One of the professor's lessons was for the class to enter an old tomb buried deep in an obscure pyramid. He gathered all the students into one of the rooms. He explained that to be a good archeologist you had to feel comfortable in close, dark places. If you couldn't handle close dark places you may want to think about another profession, Dr. Heilman told them. Then he turned out all the lights. Andrew could remember the experience as if it were yesterday. There was a chorus of gasps as the class experienced the total darkness. He could now hear the professor speaking in his German accent, "This could happen to you at any time when you are exploring these old ruins. The first thing is not to panic. I will say that again, do not panic. When the darkness has finally settled in your brain, let it sit there for at least five minutes. Do not move until your breathing has returned to normal. Count to 300 very slowly. Everyone that is thrown into total darkness unexpectedly is overcome by the experience. It doesn't matter if it happens once or a thousand times in your lifetime. You must stay in control of yourself. This is one of the major reasons I have told you to always memorize your steps into any area that does not provide natural light. Now you are all standing here. I want the first person who sees the way out to tell me."

Many of the members of the class expressed sounds of puzzlement by his statement. One of the students voice could be heard, but professor I can't see.

The rest of the class laughed. Silence, the professor said loudly. The group hushed immediately.

"Of course you can't see with your eyes. Let your mind come into play. It has no eyes but it can help you see your way out, but only if you let it. When you can see your way out, I want you to leave, and no running."

The class laughed and then stood in silence. About five minutes into the exercise, one of the students could be heard walking slowly out of the room. Ten minutes later all the students were gathered in a circle outside the darkened room silently standing together as if they had just had an epiphany.

Now, all these years later, Andrew was to go through his own exercise to find his way out of the tomb. In this case, however, when he got to his entrance, he still didn't have a way out. As Andrew stood in the room and his eyes became used to the total darkness, he realized the darkness wasn't total. There was a light source emitting from the far corner of the room. Andrew was concerned about moving through an area he had not previously explored. There could be a sink hole directly in front of him and he wouldn't know it. He would have to crawl toward the light and if there was no way large enough for his body to get to it, he would go back the way he had come.

The floor of the room was cool and damp. He couldn't put a lot of pressure on his left hand because of the broken fingers. He slowly made his way toward the light. The light was coming from the end of a long passageway. He crawled for ten minutes. He estimated the distance to be over 100 feet. He would have loved to have seen what was on the walls of the passageway he just crawled through. He imagined there were paintings of the hundreds of gods the Mayans worshiped. His knees ached and his pants were wet. He decided he needed to stand up and stretch. He wasn't sure if the ceiling of this passage was as tall as the passage he fell into. As he started to get up, his head came in contact with the ceiling. This area only had a ceiling height of a little over five feet. He stood up the best he could with his six foot frame in a five foot space. He flexed his muscles to relieve the stiffness. He continued crawling along the passageway. For the next five minutes, the light continued to become stronger. Finally, with his knees aching, he arrived at the opening. He was hoping this opening would lead directly to the surface and not be at the bottom of another ten foot sink hole. He crawled the final few feet and he could now see out of the opening. There was enough space for him to crawl out. From his vantage point he was looking directly out at the ocean. When he got to the rim of the opening he was glad to find the cave was just five feet down from the surface of the ground above him. Looking down the ocean was about twenty feet below the cave opening. The storm must have washed away at least fifty feet of the shoreline exposing the tunnel to the Mayan ruins. He was lucky the storm was so fierce or he may never have been able to get out of the cave through this newly created opening.

Andrew reached up and tugged on some exposed tree roots. They seemed strong enough to be used to pull himself up and out of the cave. The roots held and although his damaged hand ached, he managed to pull himself up to the ground above. As he lay in a grassy area, trying to catch his breath, he tried to figure out what to do next. The idea hit him. He still had the necklace with the precious stones and his knife. He looked at the beauty created by the Mayans so many long years ago. There was an inscription on the back of the medallion. It said the one who wears this medallion is to be King of all the Mayans. The mystical powers of this medallion will restore the Mayan kingdom to its original glory. The sun, moon and stars will be the handmaidens of the one who wears this medallion. Andrew thought the inscription strange. He had never seen anything like this written by the Mayans. He wished he had time to study the meaning of the message. It was getting late and he had to get back.

He hated to do this but he took the medallion and gently pried out the stones. He needed a hiding place that would not raise suspicion of the police. He took the stones and tucked them under his bandaged hand and let them rest in the palm of his hand. There was just enough room under the bandages to conceal the gems. He took the gold chain and the medallion and dropped them on the muddy ground. He hated to desecrate this old treasure but it had to be done. He stepped on the necklace and ground it into the soggy ground. After he felt he had ground enough dirt into the nooks and crannies of the medallion, he picked it up and headed back toward the dig. As he crested the hill he could see the men taking a break from bailing the water out of the trench. He yelled to them. Catching them by surprise, they jumped up and started bailing again. As he got closer they knew something had happened.

"Stop what you are doing. Come see this," Andrew said in Spanish to Raul and the men.

"I have found this necklace and a medallion on the other side of the hill. It must have been unearthed by the storm."

CHAPTER TEN

"Captain Sanchez I have something to report, over" said the policeman into the two-way radio at the site of Andrew's dig.

"This is Sanchez. What do you have to report, over?"

"That American has found a large Mayan treasure. All the men are gathering around him. I can see something very shiny. It looks like a gold necklace with a large gold circle hanging from it, over" the policeman said into the radio.

"Watch them. I will be out there as soon as I can. I want to see this for myself," Sanchez said as he got up from his pile of paperwork. He grabbed his hat and was out the door.

Sanchez needed something to give to Miguel. All the rain and storms had kept the American from their digging and Sanchez had not made any extra money for the last few weeks. *This new treasure may be the one that would keep him in good graces with the man in the big house,* Sanchez thought. He raced his police car as fast as the road would allow. He arrived at the site and went straight to the tent of the workers. Andrew was expecting him. He had seen the policeman hiding on the top of the knoll 100 yards from the site. The glare from his binoculars and the smell of his foul-smelling cigars drifted over the dig site all day long. The gems, still hidden in his bandaged hand, were starting to cut into the flesh of his palm. He needed to find another place to hide the gems soon. For now, he would put up with the pain.

Sanchez pulled up in his mud-caked Jeep and screeched to a stop. The men moved as far away as they could from him. They would rather not have the police captain see them working the dig.

"Hello American, how is everything? Have you dug up any more of our nation's treasures? The museum will need to build on a new wing with all the wonderful things you have found here. You must be proud of the things you have found for our country," Sanchez said as he swaggered into the tent.

"Captain Sanchez. What a surprise. I have just photographed my find. I will want to keep this medallion for a few days so I can carefully examine it and see if any of the Mayan gods are depicted on it," Andrew said.

"I need to see this new find," Sanchez said as he grabbed the chain and medallion out of Andrew's hand.

"This is much too valuable to let it stay in your tent. There are many poor Mexicans who would kill for something as valuable as this. I can't let you take all the responsibility for protecting this. I will take it back to my office and put it into my safe."

"I will come into town tomorrow to inspect it, if that is alright with you," Andrew said.

"Come along anytime. If I'm not there you can wait or come back the next day. I may be out of town for a day or two. Where did you find this?" asked Sanchez.

"It was lying on the ground. The storm must have washed the dirt away from it. The men were bailing out the water and I took a short walk to see what the storm had destroyed. That's when I found this in the mud."

Andrew knew Sanchez would ask the man who had been watching them to make sure his story was correct. He now had to get back to his camp and find a better place to hide the gems. They were slicing up the palm of his hand.

"How are your fingers? I see they are still bleeding. You better take care of that before you have a bad infection," Sanchez said as he was leaving the dig site with the medallion and chain tucked into a cloth bag he just happened to have with him.

Andrew looked at his blood stained bandages. He thought to himself, *if he only knew what made those bloody stains.* Andrew laughed to himself as he watched Sanchez drive away from the site.

Andrew looked at the trenches the men had cleared of water. They were slippery and soggy with wet mud. There was no way they could get down in the trenches today.

"You men did a good job but it's too muddy to go on. Tomorrow will be better. Let's call it a day and head back to the camp. I will need to go into Cancun, if any of you want to go with me."

All the men's faces lit up. They loved to go into Cancun; visit the bars, see the hot tourist women, and hot Mexican girls trying to hustle the tourists. Andrew let Raul drive back to the camp. He needed time to think of how he was going to get the stones out of Mexico and into the states.

CHAPTER ELEVEN

"It was lying on the ground, he told me," Captain Sanchez said to Miguel while standing in his house.

"When did he find this?" asked Miguel as he took out a large magnifying glass from his desk drawer.

"He found it yesterday after the hurricane."

"What did he tell you again?"

"He said he was walking over a small hill and saw it on the ground. My man who was watching him said he went for a walk and came back over the hill shouting about the find."

"Did your man tell you how long he was gone before he came back?"

"He said the American was gone for a few hours. His men were bailing water out of the trenches they had been digging. It took them two hours to finish bailing. The men were resting when the American ran back toward them."

All these questions were making Captain Sanchez start to sweat again, and he didn't bring an extra shirt with him. After looking carefully through the magnifying glass for some time, Miguel looked up and said, "There were stones or some other kind of ornament attached to this medallion. From the appearance of this necklace is hasn't been in the ground for very long. Your American has lied to you."

"How can you tell?" asked Sanchez.

"Look through the glass. See those projections there, and there, and there?"

"Yes, so what does that mean?

"They are there to hold something in place. Look at this piece of jewelry from my collection. See how similar they look, except yours is missing the stones and this one is very small in comparison."

"Yes! Yes I can see what you are saying. Those little projections hold in the stones, and this medallion has missing stones."

"There were stones on the medallion when the American found it. They are probably very valuable from the size of the projections on the medallion"

"How can you know that?" asked Sanchez wanting to know more about the jewelry.

"Look at the scratches. What do you see?"

"The scratches look like little circles," Sanchez said studying the scratches.

"That's exactly right. After your American found the medallion, he removed the stones, and if you look you can see little scratches probably from the pocket knife he used to remove them. He then dropped the medallion in the dirt and ground it into the mud to make it look as if it had been lying in the ground for a long time. When he ground the medallion into the mud little scratches were made from his foot twisting the gold into the ground. Pure gold is so soft it easily scratches," Miguel stated.

"That's amazing how you know so much by looking through this glass," Sanchez said in amazement.

Miguel read the inscription on the back of the medallion. It said the one who wears this medallion is to be King of all the Mayans. Miguel's heart started to race. This is the medallion he had been looking for. A number of years ago he had obtained a clay pot with an inscription on it that told about a boy king who had mystical powers. It was told he could fly when he wore a certain medallion. His downfall was he didn't impress the Spanish Conquistadors that came to the Mayan city looking for gold. He was shot but the people of the city were supposedly successful in hiding the body and the medallion in a secret tomb. The mystical powers of this medallion were supposedly able to restore the Mayan kingdom to its original glory. The sun, moon and stars would be the handmaidens of the one who wears this medallion. The medallion had a picture graph showing the person wearing the necklace, flying. The wearer was considered by the Mayans to be a human god. Miguel couldn't believe his luck. He needed to have the gems that had been attached to the medallion.

Miguel started talking to Sanchez, "The Mayans who lived in the area were in control of the trade routes on land and sea. One picture graph showed what looked like a Spanish war ship being captured by the Mayans. If Miguel understood this picture graph correctly the gems that were attached to the medallion represented the sun, moon and stars. I could guess since the best emeralds in the world come from Columbia, one of the stones came from there. If they indeed captured a Spanish war ship, they could have taken the treasure the Spanish had on board. My guess is there was a large ruby and diamonds or sapphires. The size of the stones would mean if they were of any reasonable quality they could be worth millions. Most people believe diamonds are the most valuable stones but that is not true. A good quality ruby can be worth many times more than the same size diamond. "

"Millions? How could he have found such a treasure and kept the gems for himself? He is an Archeologist. He couldn't intentionally desecrate a treasure like this," asked Sanchez loudly.

"This man has had everything of value taken from him. Maybe he has had enough of us. Maybe he is going to take the stones and leave our beautiful country. If he gets those stones out of the country and shows people in the United States, someone will start asking questions. He will have the officials down on your head. You will spend the rest of your life without your sweet wife, children and that cute mistress you have. We need time to search the area where our archeologist found this medallion to see if there are any more Mayan artifacts."

Sanchez was stunned. He didn't know anyone knew about Carlota. Now Miguel had something else to hold over his head. He was certainly going to go to jail. Carlota was too young to have a lover. He could spend years in the big jail in Mexico City. If the other inmates ever found out he was a policeman, he would be dead in an hour. He didn't have a chance.

"What can I do? I'll do anything to straighten this out. I don't want my wife and children, to suffer for what I have done," Sanchez pleaded to Miguel.

"If you really want to have all of this behind you, and maybe more money than you could make in two years, you are going to have to listen to me and do exactly as I say. Do I make myself clear?"

"I understand. What will I have to do?"

"You need to find those stones and then you need to make sure the American does not tell anyone about the find. There may be more treasure in that area and if we can get rid of the American, we can look for it ourselves. We could be richer than we ever dreamed. You can have ten Carlota's. You would have to start taking *Viagra,*" Miguel said and started to laugh.

Sanchez now could see there was a way out of his terrible mess. He would have to be ruthless, but he could if he had to. He had learned from Miguel. He now had to go to his men and do the same to them. He decided that he would scare them and then offer them riches greater than they could expect in their entire lifetimes. Things were looking up but he would have to be ruthless.

CHAPTER TWELVE

Andrew had gotten back to the camp and had come up with nothing in the way of a fool proof plan to get the gems out of the country. His first thought was to swallow them and head for the states. After he saw what his palm looked like from a few hours of rubbing, he could only imagine what the inside of his intestines would be like if the gems passed through. He would never have a chance to become a famous archaeologist. He would be ready for his own coffin instead of studying the one he found near the dig. He had washed, changed his cloths, and replaced his bandage. He had promised his workers he would take them to Cancun and he was ready to go. Maybe an idea would come to him on his trip into the city.

"Is everyone ready?" he asked as he left his tent to go to Cancun.

The men were standing all clean and neat. Their hair was slicked down and each man had it parted in the middle. All were dressed in their best clothes. They were standing in a line like solders ready to be inspected. Andrew couldn't help but laugh at the sight of his men all dressed up ready for a night of fun. They all piled into the truck. Raul drove and they all sang Mexican love songs to get themselves in the mood for their night ahead.

Andrew was going to go to the clinic and have one of the doctors check him out. He didn't think there was any infection. If any infection set in, being so far out of town could take too long to get to a doctor. He could lose his hand and that would be the end of his career. He also needed to find a way to get the stones out of the country. He was now hiding them in separate little pockets he had sewn into the lining of the tail of the shirt he was wearing. He figured no one would know he was carrying them.

CHAPTER THIRTEEN

"I checked with the front desk and they told me about this new American bar. Let's go check it out," said Bob.

"Where is Sam?" asked Mike.

"Out looking at some old ruins. I'll leave a note," said Mike.

The two men headed out of the hotel to walk the three blocks to the new bar on the beach. They didn't want to miss the opportunity to test a new bar. Their vacation was coming to a close and they wanted to make the most of it before they had to go back to the cold weather in Pennsylvania.

CHAPTER FOURTEEN

Andrew dropped the men off at their favorite bar. The Spanish music could be heard as the men jumped from the truck.

"I will be here to pick you up at 12:00 o'clock tonight. We are going to have a busy day tomorrow so don't drink too much," Andrew said to them in Spanish.

The men laughed as they slapped each other on the back and headed for a few drinks. Andrew drove to the doctor's office. There was no one in the clinic needing treatment at this hour but he knew after dark men would be coming in with wounds from various bar fights. He entered the clinic and was seen quickly by the practicing doctor. He looked at Andrew's fingers and re-bandaged the hand.

"How did you get those cuts on your palm?" asked the doctor.

"A broken glass in the dish water," Andrew lied.

"Change the dressing tomorrow and apply this cream. If you see any reddening come back. Those fingers should heal as long as you stop abusing them," the doctor said.

Andrew was glad his hand was doing well. Now he had to find a way to get the stones out of the country without getting caught. He decided to go to the new American bar. Maybe someone in the bar would actually be an American. He may be able to talk someone into getting the stones out of the country.

As Andrew started his truck, he looked in the rear view mirror. He spotted one of the policemen in an unmarked car. It was the policeman who had watched his dig site. Andrew drove down the street toward the American bar. The policeman was right behind him. *This is going to be more difficult than I expected,* thought Andrew as he pulled into a parking space.

CHAPTER FIFTEEN

Mike and Bob found the new American bar and walked inside. It was getting crowded. Most of the people looked to be anything but American. There was a disco atmosphere to the décor. A man playing tapes and records was dressed in sixties clothing. It must have been a problem to find the outfit he was wearing. The flared pants and the platform shoes were accented by a striped silk shirt showing the man's hairy chest. He wore a heavy gold chain, and his head was full with massive sideburns. The two almost started to laugh.

"Does it feel like we are in the middle of the 'Saturday Night Fever' movie set?" asked Mike.

"I think that's John Travolta over in the corner," laughed Bob.

"I hope Sam gets here to see this place. Sam loves 60's music," said Mike.

The two settled on two bar stools and ordered a couple of beers.

Andrew walked into the bar and looked over the crowd. Most of the tables were taken by tourists from Eastern Europe. There was a seat at the bar. He moved onto the stool and ordered an American beer. He listened to the people around him and was glad to hear the two next to him speaking English.

Andrew listened to the two men and when one of them said Somerset he had to interrupt.

"Excuse me, but I couldn't help overhearing you mention Somerset. That wouldn't be Somerset, Pennsylvania, by any chance?" asked Andrew.

"Yeah, that's where we live."

"No shit. Small world. I was born and raised there. I went to Somerset High and then on to Penn State. Let me buy you a beer," said Andrew.

After they each found out about the other, they got into who they knew, who was still in town, who got married and all the stuff people ask of a stranger that was fast becoming a friend.

Mike and Bob kept looking toward the door.

"You guys looking for someone?" asked Andrew.

"The third member of our team named Sam," replied Bob.

"Is that the third member of The Three Studs Construction Company you talked about?" asked Andrew.

"Yeah. We left a note where we were going. Sam should be here by now. We better leave and see what the problem is."

"No, wait. I have something important to talk about with the two of you. Let me buy you another beer. What I have to tell may take a while. Let's move to a table. If you are hungry I'll buy you dinner. I need some of your time and I think I can trust the two of you with what I'm about to tell you," Andrew said.

For the next hour Andrew told them the story of how everything he found was stolen. Both men became hostile toward the police in Cancun.

All the beer Bob and Mike had consumed made it easier for them to rally around a fellow American. They believed in fair play and wanted to help. The more they drank the more they wanted to help. Before long Andrew had told them of his plan and how they could help him.

Sam returned from the bus trip to the Mayan ruins with a killer headache. *The only way to get rid of it, when that happened, was to go to bed and sleep it off. Bob and Mike won't miss me, besides they probably have found a couple of girls to keep them company,* Sam thought. They surely don't need me with a bad headache to slow them down. Sam took two more aspirin and went to bed.

CHAPTER SIXTEEN

Captain Sanchez had relieved his man who was watching the American archeologist. Sanchez now sat in a dark corner of the new American bar. He tried to read the lips of the three men as they sat at the bar talking and laughing. He got the impression the archeologist had something in common with the two men he was now talking with. Who could these men be? Was it just a coincidence these men met at this bar? Sanchez didn't believe in coincidence. What could they possibly have in common? The United States is such a big place. How would he know these men and why would he trust them with maybe millions of dollars worth of rare stones? How could the archeologist just happen upon two men he knew, unless he contacted the two men to meet him here to give them the stones? That's what is happening Sanchez thought.

Captain Sanchez was confused. Americans were so unusual; they didn't act like any other people in the world. Sanchez remembered when he became involved with drug smuggling into Germany. Those people, the Germans, had no way of deviating from a plan to ship ten kilos of opium into Munich. The men followed the plan to the minute and when they realized they were being followed, they kept right on going to the drop site for the drugs. They couldn't deviate enough to keep themselves out of jail. Germans were predictable. On the other hand, you never know what Americans will do. They are so unpredictable.

Sanchez watched the men move to a table and order food. Sanchez was hungry but didn't want to be in the middle of eating if the three men decided to get up and leave. He had a drink in front of him, but it was paid for when it was delivered. He could jump up and leave at any time. He hoped his cousin Palo, who he had stationed outside to help follow anyone that left the bar, was still awake.

"Palo are you ready when I need you?" Sanchez asked into his two-way radio.

"I am. Are the three of them ready to leave the bar?" Palo asked.

"Not yet. I wanted to be sure you were ready. Call you later," Sanchez said quietly and turned off his radio.

Captain Sanchez watched the men eat and talk for a long time. He waited until Andrew was finished talking to the two men and was leaving the bar. He followed close behind as Andrew headed up the street toward his truck. Sanchez waited until Andrew was near his truck and away from any pedestrians.

"Excuse me Mister Archeologist. May I talk with you?"

Andrew turned, having already recognized the voice.

"What can I do for you Captain?" he asked.

"Why were you talking to those two *gringos* in the bar?" Sanchez asked.

"Just being friendly, that's all," said Andrew.

"You seemed to become good friends very quickly."

"They come from the same town as I do."

"What town is that?" the Captain asked.

"I don't see that's any of your business."

Sanchez struck out at those words and hit Andrew in the face with a small club he had drawn from a side pocket in his slacks. The club opened a large gash on Andrew's cheek. Sanchez did not tolerate anyone talking back to him no matter who they were.

"I am a police officer. I can ask you any questions I want. You are not a citizen of this country. I will have you thrown in jail or, if I want, I will have you thrown out of the country. I can do that if and when I want. Do you understand me?" Sanchez said as he brandished his club at Andrew.

Andrew felt his cheek open from the club smashing into it. He could feel the blood seeping from the wound.

"They are from Somerset, Pennsylvania, and are here on vacation. Do you have any other questions? I have to pick up my men in five minutes."

"You will leave when I'm ready. Your men can wait. Where are the stones?" he asked so quickly Andrew was almost thrown off guard. *How did he know there were stones?* Andrew thought.

"I just met these men and we were just talking about old times. I don't understand what stones you are talking about."

"Where are they staying in Cancun?" asked Sanchez.

"I don't know. I only met them for the first time. They are here on vacation and I heard them mention Somerset, Pennsylvania, and I started talking with them. That's all."

Sanchez swung the club again, hitting Andrew on his ear. The pain shot through Andrew's head.

He was ready to take this little bastard Sanchez down, but knew he would be put in jail until he told him about the stones. He would never get out of Mexico to get his share of the precious stones. He would probably die in a stinking jail. He had to take the abuse and deny any knowledge of the gems.

"Did you find some stones this afternoon at the place you were digging?" Sanchez asked.

"I only found a chain and medallion. There were no stones. You didn't give me enough time to study the medallion. If you think there was something of value attached to the medallion, I will start looking for them tomorrow and you are welcome to come with me if you like," Andrew said.

Sanchez thought he would never find the stones if he threw

the archeologist into jail. Miguel told him there were stones. Maybe this archeologist was telling the truth. How was Miguel so certain there were precious stones in the medallion? Maybe Miguel wanted Sanchez to keep finding treasure for him. Sanchez had to make a fast decision.

"I want to see you at the dig tomorrow morning. We will look together. I will bring a few extra men to help in the search. Now get in your truck and go get your men and clean up that cheek. You look terrible."

Sanchez walked back to his Jeep after he watched Andrew drive away. He got into his Jeep and made a call on the radio.

"Where are they?" he asked.

"Captain, they have just staggered into the Empress Hotel."

"Go inside and find out all you can about them NOW!" shouted Sanchez.

CHAPTER SEVENTEEN

"Sam, wakeup! Sam!" yelled Bob.

"What the hell do you want? I've got a hell of a headache and you aren't helping it one damn bit. What time is it?"

"It's two a.m. but that's not the problem," Bob said.

"The problem is you're drunk and I bet your brother is shit faced too. Why are you bothering me at this hour?" asked Sam.

"You aren't going to believe what happened to us in the American Bar," Bob said.

"Where is your brother?"

The question was answered as the toilet flushed. Mike came out zipping up his pants.

"I'm glad you rolled that snake into your pants before you came out here. What is your brother talking about? " asked Sam.

"Let him tell you and I'll fill in on the parts he forgets," Mike said.

"We met this guy in the bar. He is an archaeologist that is down here doing archaeological stuff. He found these big ass jewels and he gave them to us to take back to the States," said Bob.

"Are you two crazy? Do you two want to spend the rest of your lives in a Mexican jail?" Sam asked.

Sam was now wide awake and sitting up.

"How do you know he is an archaeologist and not some crook?

We have been through that before if you remember," said Sam.

"We know the guy. He's from Somerset. We played football together," Bob said.

"What's his name?"

"Andrew Kosco. He was a defensive end. He was a senior when we were freshman. He went on to Penn State and has been down here for almost two years. He has been digging in the Mayan ruins 20 miles north of here," said Bob.

"I think I know the family. They lived on the street in back of the hardware store," said Sam.

"Yeah, that's what he told us."

"He's six feet tall with light brown hair. Father worked in the mines for a while then started in the steel business. The mother worked in the school cafeteria, as I remember. He had two younger brothers."

"That's him. He told us the same stuff. His sister married and moved to California. The other two brothers work with his father in their steel business in Pittsburgh."

"Okay, get back to this thing about jewels," Sam said.

Bob reached into his pocket and pulled out a piece of cloth. There were lumps sewn into the cloth.

"What the hell is that?" Sam asked.

"The stones. He told us not to open it until we got to our hotel room, and no one is supposed to know we have them. He said if we can't get them out of the country, hide them and when we see him in a week, we will tell him where we hid them. He will try to find another way to get them out of Mexico," Bob said excitedly.

"How the hell are we supposed to do that?" Sam asked.

"We told him that you would find a way," said Mike.

"Why did you drag me into this? I don't want any part of this. If you two idiots want to believe a stranger …"

"Andrew isn't a stranger. We know the family. He lived in Somerset," interrupted Bob.

"He is a stranger to us and he wants us to break the law. If I keep going on vacation with you two, it won't take long before I will be outlawed in every damn vacation spot in the Caribbean and Central America," Sam said.

"Does that mean you will help us get these out of the country?" asked Mike.

"I haven't said yes yet. I'm thinking," said Sam.

"He said we would share in the money they bring in, fifty-fifty."

"Does that mean we share the jail time, fifty-fifty, too? Have you seen the stones?" asked Sam.

"We wanted to wait until we could all see them at the same time," Bob said as he swayed back and forth.

"Open them up," said Sam.

Mike took the old shirt tail and ripped the material. The stones cascaded on to the white sheet. None of the stones were professionally cut, but they were all polished and shined in the light from the lamp on the bed stand.

"Wow, they are beautiful!" exclaimed Bob.

"Andrew said they used to belong to a Mayan King," Mike replied.

"Those Mayans knew how to dress," Sam said.

After they all stared at the stones for some time, Mike asked, "I know how we can get them into the country. We could swallow them and shit them out when we get home."

"Don't you remember what Andrew said about how they cut his hand? They would probably cut your insides and kill you." slurred Bob.

"Oh yeah, he did tell us that. How else can we get them out? We can just put them in our pocket and walk through customs. They don't search anybody. They just look in bags for food and crap people buy in these places," Bob said.

"You would look so guilty they would have you in the back room with your pockets pulled inside out in seconds. Remember when you tried to steal that candy bar from the grocery store when you were a kid? You got out the door, turned around, started to cry, and threw the candy bar back through the doorway. You couldn't steal shit," said Sam.

"I could do it. I stole lots of stuff," said Mike.

"What have you stolen Mister Big Criminal?" asked Sam.

"I took some tools from my bricklaying class and nobody ever knew," said Mike with his eyes starting to close.

"This is a little different. Let me think about this. You two go get some sleep. You both look like shit. We still have one full day of our vacation to come up with a way to get the jewels out of the country. I need some sleep. I doubt I'll get any, but I want to try," Sam said getting back into bed.

"I will take these to my room," said Bob trying to pick up the stones to no avail.

"I think you are a little too drunk to be trusted with these. The two of you need to go straight to your rooms and I would suggest you don't even think about these stones. Meet me on the beach tomorrow at ten," said Sam, as Mike and Bob staggered out of the room.

Sam lay in bed, with the gems wrapped in a wash cloth tucked under the pillow, thinking what the hell have those two got me into this time? Somehow, Sam fell asleep and soon started to snore.

CHAPTER EIGHTEEN

Andrew managed to get the men home without any of them asking questions about his appearance. Maybe, because they all were so drunk, they didn't notice the cut on his cheek and his swollen ear. Andrew had to help most of the men get into their beds. Finally, after he got all the men settled down, he lay in his bed thinking about what he was going to do. He now had broken the law in Mexico. If he, or the Americans he gave the gems to ever got caught, they would be thrown in jail for the rest of their lives. How did Sanchez know there were stones attached to the medallion? He surely didn't come up with that piece of information on his own. Andrew sat up in bed as the thought hit him. *That bastard Hernandos must already have the necklace. It had to be Miguel who told Sanchez about the gems on the medallion. Miguel is not as dumb as I thought. I'm going to have to find out all I can about this guy. It won't be Sanchez that has me put in prison it will be that guy in the mansion. I'm sure I didn't make him happy by showing up at his door accusing him of taking Mayan treasures,* Andrew thought.

Andrew lay back down in his bed. His cheek was throbbing, his ear hurt, and his fingers were aching. He had a lot of reasons now to hate the authorities of this country and he had more reasons to hate their crooked friends. As soon as his grant to dig was over, he would be out of Mexico. He then realized he couldn't stay in this country even if he wanted to. Every move he made was being watched. If he found anything, it would be taken and given to that asshole Hernandos.

Andrew thought, *I should have found out more about that guy before I went to his house. That was my big mistake. All I knew about Miguel was that he had a lot of money and his last name was Hernandos.*

If Andrew ever expected to get out of Mexico alive, he had better come up with a plan. He had to find some way to protect himself from these crooks. If he were ever to end up in court, it was his word against theirs. He had sent reports home to the States but since he wanted to publish a book on his findings, he had kept all his notes and pictures with him. He needed to get some of the pictures and notes back to the States. He realized he had made a mistake by not sharing his findings with other Archaeologists back in the states. He would have to rectify that as soon as possible. Andrew decided to get the papers together in the morning and send them back to the University for safe keeping. Maybe then he would have something to use if Sanchez and Hernandos decided they had stolen all that they could and he had become a liability. Andrew finally started to feel a little more at ease. He had formulated a plan that could keep him alive. He needed to share what he knew with Penn State. Tomorrow would be a very busy day. He needed to get some sleep. He finally drifted off, but continued to wake up with every turn of his body as his cheek, ear, or fingers would start to ache.

Morning came too quickly, but Andrew was feeling better about making it through the mess that the dig had created. He went to his computer and faxed some of his findings back to the States.

CHAPTER NINETEEN

Sam was enjoying a better day. The headache was gone and this was the last full day they were going to be in Cancun. Not looking forward to the snow in Pennsylvania, Sam put on a pair of shorts, and went down to breakfast. The eggs, bacon, toast, and three cups of coffee went down easily. As Sam sat reading the newspaper, a couple at the next table was discussing some jewelry purchases they had just made.

"Isn't it amazing how inexpensive this stuff is down here? We can do next year's Christmas shopping right here. The man at the store told me we had to keep the sales slips handy and pack all the presents in a separate bag. We then tell the man at the immigration desk so we wouldn't be held up at all. They want us to buy this stuff. It's a big money maker for their economy. I just can't believe how inexpensively they can make this stuff. The gems on this necklace look real!" the woman exclaimed.

Her husband said disgustedly, "They don't pay their workers anything, that's how they do it. There aren't any unions down here. You can be sure of that. That's why all of them are trying to sneak across the border to our country," the man said going back to reading the sports section of his newspaper.

Sam's ears perked up. Looking over at the jewelry the woman had purchased, Sam asked the husband, "Excuse me, I couldn't help overhearing you talk about the good prices you got on the jewelry. Would you mind telling me where you bought it?"

"Down the street on the left. I don't remember the name of the shop but you can't miss it. They have a guy outside grabbing people off the street to buy their stuff. My wife didn't need much prodding to get her into the store, if you know what I mean," the husband said nudging Sam with his elbow.

Sam finished the remaining swallow of coffee, paid the bill, and was out the door in a flash. The jewelry store was easy to find. A man in an orange tee shirt was handing out discount coupons for ten percent off to everyone who walked by. At every chance he got, he escorted a potential customer into the shop. Sam grabbed a coupon from the man and went inside without the need of an escort. The place was full of tourists looking for bargains. Sam didn't know anything about the silver jewelry the shop was selling. The only criteria were to find a few pieces that would have stones the size of the ones they were going to get back into the United States.

"May I help you?" the salesperson asked.

"I want that one, that one there, and the one in the far corner. How much?" Sam asked.

"Seventy-five American dollars," the salesperson said.

Sam handed the 10% off coupon to the salesperson.

"This coupon isn't for these items. It is only good for the items in that basket," she said as she pointed to a small basket in the corner.

Sam gave a disgusted look and started to walk out of the store. The sales person yelled, "Wait, I will make an exception. You seem to know the good pieces from the everyday jewelry. I'll take that coupon," she said as she reached for the piece of paper Sam was holding in an outstretched hand."

The purchase was made. Sam carefully tucked the sales slip away, took the package and headed for the beach where Mike and Bob were sitting in the sun.

CHAPTER TWENTY

"Captain Sanchez we have followed the two men since they left the hotel. They have been on the beach and look like they are going to stay there for a while," reported the policeman who was following Bob and Mike.

"Stay with them. Let me know if they leave," Sanchez said as he drove to the dig site.

Sanchez had learned nothing new about the men from Pennsylvania. His men questioned the woman at the desk in the hotel last night. All the policemen found out was the two men who met Andrew at the bar were from Somerset, Pennsylvania, and they were going to be leaving tomorrow. Sanchez was almost certain if there were any stones, one or both of the men from Somerset had them. Yet, Sanchez still wasn't really sure if the archeologist ever found stones in the medallion.

Miguel called Sanchez this morning and wanted to know if he had found the stones yet. He had to tell Miguel something. He still wasn't sure there ever were any stones, yet he had to believe Miguel.

Sanchez parked the Jeep at the dig site and approached the tent of the archeologist. He planned on following Andrew all day. He would also need to search everything in his tent. He had to find out about the possibility of there being any stones.

Sanchez entered the tent without announcing himself. Andrew was changing the dressing on his hand. Sanchez stood by the entrance of the tent with his thumbs tucked in the black police belt. Andrew thought Sanchez was trying to look like a tough American cowboy.

"I will follow you, but first I have to make an important call about a police matter. Start without me," he said as Andrew left the tent and started to climb into the truck to go to the dig site.

The truck full of men and equipment started down the muddy road. Sanchez waited until the truck was out of site before he entered Andrew's tent. He searched everywhere but had no success finding any stones from a Mayan Medallion. He didn't think the American was stupid enough to leave them in the tent but he had to check to make sure.

Sanchez finished his search and headed to the dig site.

"Where did you walk yesterday and where was the medallion found?" asked Sanchez as he walked up to Andrew at the dig site.

"The men were cleaning the remaining water out of the trench and I went this way," said Andrew as he pointed over a small hill.

Sanchez and Andrew started walking in the direction he had taken yesterday. After he walked over the ridge and out of sight of where the police officer was watching yesterday, Andrew veered to the right. He wanted to keep Sanchez clear of the sink hole and the buried Mayan temple.

Andrew was pretty sure Sanchez was not in very good shape for walking over the hills and valleys of the area so he picked up the pace. Andrew noticed the fancy boots Sanchez was wearing and thought a little dirt on his spit shined boots would be good for him. They walked quickly for twenty minutes. Sanchez was getting out of breath. The extra twenty pounds he had gained over the past year was slowing him down. Andrew picked up the pace for five more minutes constantly looking for somewhere that would be a plausible location for finding treasure. He chanced upon a piece of pottery sticking out of the soft earth. He stopped to let Sanchez catch up.

"Here is the spot. Look! I think that is a piece of pottery."

Sanchez finally caught up with Andrew. Sanchez's shirt was heavily stained with sweat. Mud had caked his once shiny boots and he was totally out of breath.

"Where?" puffed Sanchez.

"There," Andrew pointed to the piece on the ground.

Sanchez went over to the piece of pottery. To both Andrew's and Sanchez's amazement it was the edge of a vessel buried in the mud and dirt. Sanchez started to pull it out of the ground.

"Stop! We have to take a picture and brush away the dirt. There may be other artifacts in the area and we want to be sure we catalog each piece," exclaimed Andrew.

Sanchez stopped tugging. Andrew carefully brushed and dug the dirt away from the artifact. The pot was approximately 6 inches wide and 9 inches long.

"This looks like a cooking pot. It's hard to find these intact. I'm glad you stopped pulling on it. The museum in Mexico where you send everything that I have found, would have been very upset if you had broken it," Andrew said sarcastically.

After they successfully extracted the cooking pot they continued to look for artifacts. Sanchez was very proud of himself for finding the pot. It was a beautiful pot and he wanted to keep it for himself. He carefully picked it up.

"You can leave it here and we will pick it up on the way back," Andrew said.

"I will carry it. I have never found a Mayan treasure before. Andrew walked further and further away from the temple site. He knew Sanchez was getting tired from the long walk. The cooking pot Sanchez carried seemed to get heavier and heavier with each step. Cradling it against his shirt had made a large mud spot on his now soaked shirt.

"I have seen enough. There are no Mayan stones here. It is getting hot and it is time to turn back. We had better work our way back to the dig site," Sanchez said.

He had been walking for an hour. His feet were hurting. He should have changed into a better pair of walking shoes instead of his military dress boots. His normally spit-shined boots were caked with mud. He would need to get one of the men to give them a good cleaning when he got back to his office and he would have to get another shirt. The sun was now out full and bright. The temperature had risen at least 20 degrees since they started. Sanchez couldn't look at the ground anymore for lost treasure. He was tired, his head hurt, his eyes were nearly blinded from looking at the bleached ground, and he needed a drink of tequila. Andrew finally carried the pot back to the dig wrapped in a cloth. As they walked back Sanchez looked over at Andrew and said, "Your shirt tail is all ripped. You should throw that old rag away."

"I like this shirt. It's my lucky shirt," Andrew said.

How could a shirt be lucky? thought Sanchez as they continued walking back to the dig site.

CHAPTER TWENTY-ONE

Captain Sanchez had assigned a policeman to watch Bob and Mike on the beach. It was boring work and the policeman was getting hungry and had to pee. He used his police radio and called into the police station for someone to relieve him. There was no one who could come out for the next hour. He decided it wouldn't hurt if he left the two of them on the beach by themselves. After all he was Captain Sanchez's cousin and some day he would be the Captain of the police force. He needed to start making his own decisions. He hitched his heavy police belt. The belt didn't fit over his large stomach. As soon as he hitched it up it was right back down where it originally was. He needed a break and it only made sense to enjoy his break the best he could. He got back in the police car and drove to a small café where he knew the pretty waitress. As the policeman started down the street to the café, Sam came up to the beach and found Bob and Mike.

"Hey you two, how are you feeling today? Don't tell me. From the looks of you two, you feel like hell."

"How could you guess?" Bob said as he tried to lift his head off the lounge chair he was lying on.

"I have a solution to your problem."

The two huddled around Sam. The three pieces of jewelry were displayed.

"What the hell are we going to do with those?" Bob asked.

"You idiot. Look at them. Those phony stones are the same size as the ones we have to take back to the States," Mike said as he picked up each piece of jewelry and examined it.

"You are pretty fast for a drunk," Sam replied.

"I just wanted to show you how we are going to get the gems into the country. All we have to do is replace the stones and declare the pieces as gifts. No one will be the wiser and if they are, we will say we didn't know. What do you think?" asked Sam. The two agreed but left Sam to do the switch of the stones. Sam headed back to the hotel leaving Bob and Mike to continue nursing their hangovers.

Sam passed a police car as it came to a halt near the beach. The policeman inside had no idea Sam was related to the two he was told to watch. The policeman was now full of food and content after his noon meal. He couldn't see any change in the two men sleeping in the lounge chairs on the beach. He settled back to continue his vigil. The phone in the police car rang.

"Patrolman Roberto here. No sir, everything here is the same. The two men are sleeping on the beach. No sir, I am fine. I don't need a break. I will stay with them until they go back to their hotel. Thank you, sir, I try to do my job as best as I can," the policeman said proudly then belched after he hung up the phone.

CHAPTER TWENTY-TWO

"Boarding for Flight 237 to Pittsburgh, Pennsylvania, United States, at Gate 4 will begin in ten minutes," said the voice over the loudspeaker in English then again in Spanish.

Mike and Bob had rushed to the gate while Sam returned the rental car.

"Next time one of you gets the car. This is a pain in my ass to have to take it to the other end of the airport," said Sam loudly.

"We'll hold the plane," Mike said as he headed into the terminal.

The policeman who had been following them made sure he kept the two men now rushing through the terminal in sight.

Sam dropped off the car and made it back to the terminal with two minutes to spare. The carry-on bag held the three necklaces with the newly mounted stones. *This would be the test. There was no line in customs check-in,* Sam thought. The necklaces were packed separately with their sales slip and paperwork from the store. The Customs Agent looked at Sam's ticket and then at the clock on the wall. Realizing Sam didn't have much time to make the flight, he didn't spend any time looking at the jewelry.

"Do you have anything else to declare?" asked the agent.

"No sir, that's all I bought."

"You should have allowed more time to get to your plane," said the agent.

"Tell my brothers. I had to take the car back and drop them off at the door."

"You should have had them come through customs with the gifts."

"If I had left it to them they would have screwed it up somehow," Sam said to the agent.

Sam arrived at the gate as it was ready to close. Mike and Bob were no where in sight. Sam handed over the ticket and went down the ramp to the plane.

The policeman assigned to Mike and Bob watched a last minute straggler board the plane. He watched as the plane left the gate and taxied out toward the runway.

The policeman thought about how well he had handled his first big assignment watching the two Americans. It wouldn't be long before he would be taking over the police force after his cousin, the Captain, retired.

The policeman needed to take a pee and he was getting hungry. As he stood peeing into the urinal he again thought about how well he was doing his job. Looking into the mirror as he washed his hands he couldn't help wondering how rich he would become as the Captain of the police force.

CHAPTER TWENTY-THREE

Sanchez put the urn he had found into his Jeep for safe keeping. He decided that since he found the urn he would keep it for himself. He deserved to have his own treasure. The Archeologist had found many urns over the past two years that he had given to Miguel or the Museum. This one was something special. He found it himself. He would have to go out more often and look for treasure. If he found out the urn was valuable he would search for more. He could always use a little more money selling his own found treasures.

It was time to check in with his cousin who was watching the two Americans. They were scheduled to leave Cancun, tonight at ten pm. He would have to get the two Americans down to the station on some charge or other so he could search their room and find the stones. He wanted to finish with the Archeologist by noon so he could work on the two Americans from Pennsylvania that afternoon. Sanchez had to make sure he handled the Americans carefully. He didn't want too many people knowing about his antiquities stealing. He had to get the stones back and then he had to get the Americans out of the country without them making any noise about the gems. He may have to detain them long enough for them to realize if they didn't keep quiet they may be held in his jail for a real long time. The Americans could get their government involved and that is the last thing Sanchez wanted. He had to be careful that no officials became interested in what was going on in his province. Maybe he would find the gems, get his share of the money, and possibly move to Mexico City. Everything was getting too complicated here. He could work for Miguel as a bodyguard or something. He was sure Miguel could find something for him to do. He then remembered Miguel's bodyguards. Miguel had offered the use of his two bodyguards if he needed them to help with the Americans. He didn't want Miguel's men too close. They would report back to Miguel on the kind of operation he was running. If Miguel didn't like the way he was running things then he may never be able to get a job working for him. He would be happy to rid himself of this police job and all his relatives. He had enough trouble with all the relatives he had working for him. The wives always wanted their husbands to ask him for more money. Maybe if he worked for Miguel, life would be a lot easier.

Sanchez had to get his mind back to the current problem. He picked up the car phone and called.

"What are the two men doing?" asked Captain Sanchez to his Cousin who was watching his two suspects.

As the policeman was eating his lunch in the airport terminal he replied, "They just left," he said while chewing a mouthful of food.

"They just left for where?" asked Sanchez.

"For America, he replied still chewing."

"That can't be! There flight was for tonight. They can't be out of the country! They have the stones!" Sanchez yelled into the phone.

"Cousin, you didn't tell me about any stones. What should I do?" asked the policeman.

Sanchez was furious. He slammed the phone into its holder on the dashboard. The phone fell to the floor in three pieces.

Sanchez was so mad he picked up the pieces, threw them out the window. He ripped the rest of the phone off the dashboard and threw it out of the car window too.

Sanchez sat in the car so furious he couldn't think. He smashed the dashboard with his fist time and again. Finally using up the uncontrolled emotions inside him, he sat still and felt the aching start to build in his fist. As control of his emotions finally gripped him he asked himself, how did they change their tickets without my knowing it? He thought the two of them were on the beach or drinking beer, or sleeping. They were watched all the time. They never went close to the travel agency. They couldn't have exchanged their tickets without taking their tickets to the travel agent. My men would have seen them. Sanchez wanted to call his cousin that was watching the two Americans and verify exactly what the two men did yesterday but the phone was in pieces on the ground. He started to lose control again. Feeling the burning in his fist reminded him to stay in control. Sanchez would have to tell Miguel about this. He wasn't going to be happy. Miguel was sure they had the stones and now he believed they had them too.

Sanchez stormed out of his Jeep and went into the tent. Andrew was standing looking at a piece of pottery his diggers had found. With his gun now drawn Sanchez shouted at Andrew, "Where are the stones?"

"What stones are you talking about?" asked Andrew still examining the pot.

Sanchez smashed his gun against the side of Andrew's face. Andrew had been hit by this guy three times in the last two days. His temper boiled over. Even looking down the muzzle of a gun, he couldn't control himself. He struck out with his fist. He hit Sanchez square in the nose. The blood shot in all directions. Sanchez had been in plenty of fights and knew when his nose was broken, and this time his nose surely was. His instincts took over before his common sense returned.

He pulled the trigger of his gun. The bullet found its mark.

Andrew fell to the ground with the Mayan pot shattering on the ground. The noise echoed in the air like a rock through a pane of glass. The men were in the trench digging. They stopped dead in their tracks. They were frozen. They knew when they heard a gunshot that the best thing to do was go the other way as fast as they could. This was different. The shot had come from the boss's tent. They knew the sheriff was in there with him. What could have provoked the Captain to shoot? They wanted to go find out what happened, but their instincts wouldn't let any of them move. Most of the men crouched down to make sure they weren't exposed to a possible second shot. They stayed waiting.

Sanchez finally regained some of his composure. Andrew was lying on the ground with blood oozing from a large hole in his chest. Sanchez stood there feeling better that now he didn't have to put up with this smart ass American. He knew that some day this was how it would end between the two of them. He just didn't expect it to end this soon. He was not ready for this to happen. Now there would be no easy ride to the wealth he wanted. He needed to tell the men outside something to cover up the shooting.

"Raul, come quickly," Captain Sanchez shouted, "Your employer has been shot. He punched me and tried to take my gun. Look, he broke my nose."

"Why did he try to take your gun Captain?" asked Raul.

"I said to him the man at the Museum in Mexico City, told me there were stones in the medallion when it was found and I should look for them. I told the American I had to take him into town to question him. He attacked me. He must have the stones around here somewhere. He was probably going to leave the country with our nation's treasures. The gun went off during our struggle. We need to get him to a doctor. Take the truck and get Doctor Perez from the clinic quickly."

"Maybe we should take him into town. By the time I get back he could be dead," said Raul.

"That is good. Let me help you put him in the truck," said Sanchez.

"My men will put him in the truck. They will go with me to care for him along the way."

Raul was off with the men and Andrew in less than a minute.

As the truck was leaving, Sanchez thought he would have made sure Andrew was dead before he could see the doctor. Raul shouldn't have gotten in the way. Sanchez would have to hope the bullet did its job without any additional help. *I'm going to have to have a talk with Raul,* thought Sanchez. *He was taking the Archeologist's side in this when he should have been thinking of a fellow countryman. He will be out of a job now that there will not be any more digging out here. I'm sure when his money starts running out he will be looking for another job. We then will see how his big mouth will help him. Now, I had better make a more thorough search of the place for those stones. If they aren't here, I'll have to follow the men from America back to their home. Those stones have to be found,* thought Sanchez.

CHAPTER TWENTY-FOUR

"We did it," Bob whispered to the other two.

"What do you mean we? You didn't do shit," said Sam.

"You know what I mean. We are out of Mexico and we still have the you-know-what's" whispered Bob.

"We have to declare them to the U.S. Customs. They are a lot smarter than those guys in Mexico. They want people to take that junk jewelry out of the country. They make lots of money from that crap," said Sam.

"By the way, you each owe me twenty-five dollars," Sam continued.

"For what?" Mike asked.

"For the junk jewelry. I'm not paying the whole bill myself," Sam said.

Bob reached into his wallet mumbling, "Couldn't you find anything cheaper?" asked Mike.

Sam and Bob laughed. Mike realized the joke and joined them in their laughter.

CHAPTER TWENTY-FIVE

Miguel was again having a fitful sleep. His long-dead mother entered his dreams and talked to him. He became depressed remembering what Sanchez had told him the night before about the shooting of the Archeologist. He had been having the best months of his life with all the new treasures the Archeologist had contributed to his collection of Mayan art. Miguel had been a Mayan art collector most of his life. When he was growing up in the streets of Mexico City, with only his mother as family, she would tell him stories of their Mayan ancestors. She told him he was from Royal Mayan blood. Some day he would have to find a way to restore his family name to a prominent place in Mexican history. She told him his true Mayan name was Texacia, which translated meant King of the Land of the Caves. He loved her stories. They made him feel important. His mother made the stories so real he knew deep in his heart and soul they were true. The stories helped push him on to find ways to gather Mayan artifacts. For a boy without formal education there was only the education of the streets. His mother died when he was twelve years old. He pushed himself on with his life and her dream of him becoming the one to unite the Mayans. To become rich enough to acquire his ancestral treasures, he became ruthless in every money making scheme he was involved in. He started by stealing anything of value and reselling it. He built an empire on illegal activities. To reach the top he had to push out of the way many men that were much older and stronger than he. His ruthlessness soon made him a feared man. He became rich as well as feared in Mexico City.

Miguel did not go to school but he was an intelligent man. He learned to read and write on his own. He read everything written on the Mayan people. He held his passion for Mayan art deep inside. He started to collect Mayan art reproductions and felt each one he owned was part of his families past glories.

One day when he was working at his illegal fencing operation, a man came in who owed him a substantial amount of money. Miguel told the man that if he didn't come up with the cash soon, he would be dead. He came into Miguel's office and offered to give him a treasure he had stolen from a rich man's home. It was an original urn found in a Mayan ruin. The man showed Miguel the urn. When Miguel touched it, something happened to him. He was transported back through the centuries. He felt he was in a Mayan city and he was their King. He had a hard time letting go of the urn. He knew he needed to have more of the real treasures of "his" people. From then on he only collected authentic relics from the Mayan civilization.

The thief was told if he came across any more Mayan art, Miguel would be interested. From then on, anyone in the city who stole Mayan art knew Miguel would buy for top dollar. With every piece of art he possessed, Miguel fell deeper and deeper into his Mayan past. Now, because of Captain Sanchez, his greatest source of original Mayan treasure had been taken from him. He would have to find another source, but first he had to find the jewels that had been taken from the medallion.

Miguel walked into his special room where he kept many of the most important Mayan treasures. He picked up the medallion. It had taken him hours to clean the dirt from all the grooves. He loved holding the medallion and chain. He considered it his most prized Mayan treasure. He could feel its power, but he knew the power was not complete. It needed the gems that had been taken from it. Miguel's inner spirit needed to have the medallion whole again. As he stood in his treasure room, he looked at all the urns and stone objects of art made by his ancestors. He felt transformed back to the days of the great Mayan civilization. He placed the necklace around his neck. As the medallion lay against his chest he could feel the energy of the Mayan people come alive. He felt the power of the medallion. He was suddenly flying through the air and being transported back in time. He was now standing on top of a pyramid during one of the five holy days of the Mayan year. It was the time for human sacrifices. He was standing in the robes of a Mayan priest. His flowing white robe flared in the breeze. Blood dripped from his hands. His robes were stained with the blood of warriors sacrificed to the powerful Mayan gods. He held a solid gold ceremonial dagger in his hand. In front of him lay a naked virgin tied to a stone alter. The alter was stained with the blood of thousands of past sacrifices. He chanted a prayer to the Mayan gods for acceptance of his sacrifice. Her drugged body lay on the alter ready to be the next victim of the slaughter. He plunged the dagger deep into her chest. With a few well practiced cuts, out came the still beating heart. He placed the pulsating heart upon the altar. Her blood flowed down the altar to mingle with gallons of blood from other human sacrifices that preceded her. As Miguel continued to pray for the gods to accept the human blood, other sacrifices stood in line to be the next token to the insatiable gods.

Miguel suddenly came out of his trance. He was shaken by the experience. The experience was so real he had to look at his hands and clothes to see if there was any blood on them. The feeling he had had was so real, and he was surprised to find out there wasn't any blood.

He wanted to feel the power again. He knew it wouldn't happen again until he found the gems and reunited them with his medallion. He knew the Archeologist had taken them and he had to have them back at any cost. He would go to the hospital to see the Archeologist. He would make him tell him where the gems were. He would have those gems. He had to have those gems. Maybe then he would be free of the dreams of his mother calling to him and telling him he would be the new leader of the Mayan people. If he would do what his mother had said to him so many times in his dreams he could bring back the power of the Mayans.

CHAPTER TWENTY-SIX

The plane landed in Pittsburgh. Snow was falling but the three didn't notice. They were concerned about getting the gems through customs. Mike and Bob went through first. Their bags were searched and the Customs Agent waved for Sam to come next.

"Go get the car and I'll meet you in front of the terminal," Sam told them.

Sam knew the two of them would look so nervous that the customs agent would surely suspect something was wrong. The two took off, as if staying there would have them in prison by nightfall.

"Anything to declare?" asked the woman checking the bags.

"I have some jewelry in this bag. The sales receipt is in there with the purchases," Sam said.

The Customs Agent unwrapped the three necklaces.

"These are the nicest stones I've seen. Where did you get these?" she asked.

Sam told her and showed the name on the sales slip.

"Their quality has improved," she said.

"That's why I bought them. I think the family is going to love them," said Sam.

"You have good taste," the Customs Agent said as she wrapped them carefully and put them back in the bag."

"Next," said the agent.

The sweat running down Sam's back wasn't seen by the Customs Agent, thank God.

CHAPTER TWENTY-SEVEN

"I have searched their room. I am sure they have the stones," Sanchez said on his cell phone to Miguel.

"How do you know for sure?" he asked.

"I found some colored glass in the trash. They must have replaced the glass with the real jewels."

"Good work. I am on my way to see you. I will be there in an hour. I want to see those stones and then we are going to the hospital to see our archeologist friend. He is still alive isn't he?" asked Miguel.

"Yes he is. The doctors told me he is in a coma and they are not sure he will pull through. I have a guard at the door to the room. Only the doctors are allowed in."

"Good. I will see you soon. Call the guard and tell him he can leave. There is no reason to keep a man at the door. I'm sure you have other things for him to do."

The hospital was more like a clinic than a full fledged health care center. The policeman had left the door to the room by the time Miguel and Captain Sanchez arrived.

Sanchez and Miguel entered. Andrew was lying on the bed with tubes in both arms and oxygen in his nose. He was pale and his breathing was shallow and labored. The skin under his fingernails was slightly blue. He didn't move as they approached the bed. As the men were standing by the bed the doctor came in.

"Is he going to live?" asked Sanchez.

"We can't tell for certain. The bullet is lodged near his heart. To remove the bullet from its location requires special equipment and we don't have the equipment here to operate. We will have to fly him to Mexico City, if we can get him stabilized," the doctor said.

The doctor looked at the chart attached to the end of the bed, made a few notes, and left the room.

"Let me see those pieces of glass you found in the hotel room," asked Miguel.

Sanchez reached in his pocket and pulled out the handful of glass.

"If the real stones are of the same size, they would be worth a lot of money," Sanchez said as he handed the stones to Miguel.

Miguel gave Sanchez a menacing look and said, "The real stones belong to me and my people. Those stones belong to me! I will restore them to the medallion. With those stones, I will become the next great leader of the Mayan people."

Sanchez just looked at Miguel. He thought the man was talking crazily. *The stones are just stones. They may be worth a lot of money but they are still just stones,* Sanchez thought

"What do you want me to do?" asked Sanchez.

"It is very simple, find them. I want to know where they are and I will come and collect them myself. I don't want you to do anything but find them."

"But from all appearances they are in the United States. In a place called Somerset, Pennsylvania."

"Then go there and locate them. I will give you $100,000 when I get the stones back. I must have those stones," Miguel said with a crazed look on his face.

Sanchez couldn't believe what he just heard. That would be enough money for him to never have to work again. He could live like a king. To hell with being a policeman, he could be rich.

"I will need some money to get to Pennsylvania and I will need someone to help me," Sanchez said.

"I want you to leave as soon as possible."

"I can leave in two days and I will call you when I have found the stones," Sanchez declared.

As he pulled a roll of American hundred dollar bills from his pocket Miguel said, "Here is $10,000. You will leave tomorrow and take your cousin with you. I don't expect anything but success."

The two men continued to look down at the comatose body of Andrew. Miguel turned and picked up a pillow lying on a chair. He removed the oxygen from Andrew's nose, placed the pillow over the mouth of Andrew and held it there until no breathing could be detected. He returned the pillow to the chair and placed the oxygen back into Andrew's nose.

"I expect you to find the stones and call me immediately." He walked out of the room. Sanchez stood there stunned as the green line on the monitor went straight and the numbers read zeros. The door closed quietly behind Miguel.

CHAPTER TWENTY-EIGHT

"How is our price for the work you want done?" Sam said to Jon at the Inn.

"Yours is the best of the three estimates I've received. When can you get started?" asked Jon.

"We can get started immediately. It will take a week to get all the materials but there are some things we can start working on now. We can talk about the details later. I'll have some drawings and material samples for you by the end of the week," Sam said.

"Sound good to me," Jon replied.

"By the way, we are expecting to have a friend we met in Cancun come to the Inn to stay for a few days. Do you have any rooms available?" asked Sam.

"The weekends are booked but we do have a few rooms during the week. When do you expect him? It is a *him* isn't it?" asked Jon.

"Yes. He is an archeologist working just outside of Cancun. He used to live here in Somerset, but now lives in Pittsburgh and works through Penn State. I expect he will be here in a few days."

"What's his name, I may know the family?" said Jon.

"His name is Andrew Kosco. He lived down by the Hardware store."

"There was one brother and a sister in the family as I remember," said Jon.

"There were two other brothers along with the sister. Their mother died and their father couldn't manage them as well as run his steel mill in Pittsburgh. Their aunt lived here and took the boys in." The brothers now live in Pittsburgh and run the steel mill. The sister is in California. That's what I was told," Sam said.

"How did you meet him?" asked Jon.

"Mike and Bob met him in a bar in Cancun. He wants to come back for a visit. Bob, Mike, and I are going to meet him here. We can try out your new bar. It looks great, by the way. You never told me who did the work?" asked Sam.

"You know you guys were going to bid on the job but I guess you got too busy with those houses to put in a bid." said Jon.

"I hired a contractor from Pittsburgh."

"If you have time I'll buy you a drink," said Sam to Jon.

"I sure could use a drink after the day I've had and you can tell me about your trip. I wish I had the time to take a vacation," Jon said as they headed for the bar.

CHAPTER TWENTY-NINE

Miguel and Captain Sanchez left the clinic. Sanchez was still shaken from watching Miguel kill Andrew. He should have arrest him on the spot. *He murdered a man right in front of my eyes,* thought Sanchez. That makes me an accomplice since I did nothing to stop him. There was no way he could have ever gotten Miguel to trial. Miguel would have had him killed in an instant. There was no doubt in his mind. He would be dead if he even inferred any wrong doing on Miguel's part. Now Miguel would forever tell Sanchez what to do and when to do it. He would have to do some serious thinking about the direction of his life after this episode with the stones is finished.

"I expect to hear from you every day, no make that twice a day, when you are in the States," Miguel said to Sanchez as he got into his limousine.

"I will call you as soon as I arrive." Sanchez said solemnly.

"What is the name of the place you are staying again?" asked Miguel.

The place written on a note pad in the archeologist's office was, The Inn at Somerset. My cousin found information in the computer. It's what the Americans call a Bed and Breakfast. The picture in the computer shows a beautiful mansion. It's not as beautiful as your *casa* but it looks very nice. Since two of the men might recognize me, I'm staying at a motel very close to the Inn," Sanchez said.

"Good, call me if you need more money. Let me know when you find the stones. I expect results and I don't want any interference from the police in the States. If you get into trouble, it will be up to you to get yourself out of it. If any of this gets back to implicate me, I will make sure, personally, that every member of your family has a pillow over their face like our friend in the clinic. I hope you understand," Miguel said calmly.

Sanchez stood in front of the police station as Miguel's limousine drove away.

"What have I gotten myself into?" he said out loud as he slinked back to his Jeep.

CHAPTER THIRTY

"Three Studs Construction Company. Oh, hi Mike, where are you?" asked Bob.

"I'm at the Inn. I found a deal on some two-by-fours and I thought I would buy them and get them to the Inn before it started to snow again," Mike said.

"It seems like a long time ago we were sitting on the beach in Cancun," Bob said as he put his feet up on his desk, "With all those half-naked women, the beer, and Tequila."

"Enough of that! It's only been two days. We have a lot of work to do and I don't want to hear you babbling about vacation. I'm freezing my ass off and there is still a lot of winter left. Get out to the shed and bring some eight and ten penny nails over here. Some of the areas in the basement are empty, and we can get some of the work done if we move our butts."

"Ten-four, I'll be there in a few minutes. Hey before I forget, do you know if Jon has heard anything from Andrew? These gems are going to burn a hole in my pocket if we have to hold on to them any longer," Bob said, still sitting with his feet up on the desk.

"Jon hasn't said anything. I was thinking the same thing. It's been two days and we haven't heard a word. Where is Sam?" he asked.

"Sam called this morning. Seems there is a flu bug going around. Sam is in bed and sounded like Lou Rawls. It may take a couple of days before that flu subsides. Hope we don't get it. We can handle the job for a few days. We can't do any major woodwork without our carpenter. I think we will have to plow along."

"Okay. Get over here. I need your help unloading," Mike said as he hung up the phone.

CHAPTER THIRTY-ONE

"Captain it's so damn cold. I don't know why you brought me on this trip," Captain Sanchez's cousin Palo said over the cell phone.

"You are here because you had a passport and you can speak English without a heavy Spanish accent, that's why."

"I'm sorry I ever went to that Catholic school. I would have been better off broke and warm back home," Palo whined.

"Stop your griping. You will be home a lot sooner if you help find the stones these two *gringo's* stole. Where are you now?" asked Sanchez.

"I am at a place called The Inn at Somerset. There is a man with a truckload of lumber. He was making a call. He probably wants some help unloading it," Palo said., as he rubbed his ears trying to get some circulation in them.

I have an idea. Go into the Inn and see if they need anyone to work for them," Sanchez said.

"Why do I want to do that? I have a job and I don't want to be in the United States any longer than I have to."

"Just listen. We need to have someone on the inside. I can't go inside because the two men may have seen me in the bar in Cancun when they were with Andrew. They would get suspicious if they see me. I don't think they know about the death of the Archeologist yet. We need to take care of this matter as soon as possible and you may not have to work there for more than a day or two."

"What kind of job should I ask for?" Palo asked.

"What can you do?" asked Sanchez getting pissed off with the conversation.

"I can wash dishes, I can clean. I can wait tables. That's all I have ever done besides being a policeman."

"You answered your own question. Now go in there and get a job. Besides, it will keep you out of the cold. Don't tell them you are a policeman or ever worked as a policeman. Do you understand?"

CHAPTER THIRTY-TWO

Miguel wasn't sleeping at all. He wanted those jewels. He wanted to be the next great king of the Mayans. At night he would drink himself into a stupor hoping he would be able to sleep. Every time he would drift off he would start dreaming about walking in a piazza back in the great Mayan city. He wasn't royalty. He was wearing rags instead of fine garments. He was not a king. He was the man cleaning up the dung from the animals that were walking the streets. He was a slave. He was spit on and kicked out of the way by the passing nobles. They would curse at him if he got too close. The dung left a stench on his skin, hair and the old rags he had for clothing. He was the lowest human life in the city. He could only take their punishment; there was nothing he could do. He was totally humiliated. He screamed out loud. In his dream, someone would kick him out of the way as they passed by on the street.

He woke up in a cold sweat. His body was still in dire need of rest, but rest would not come. He blamed his predicament on the loss of the stones. If he had them he would be a real king, not a lowly slave. He needed those stones. He was now obsessed with having them.

He had heard from Captain Sanchez twice a day for the two days he had been gone. He wanted Sanchez and his cousin to find the stones instantly and to tell him where they were, so he could fly up and take them back to his home. He wanted to feel the medallion around his neck with the stones in their rightful places. He had taken the phony glass that was discarded by the American thieves and tried to put them into the medallion. For some reason the stones would not stay in place. Miguel got one stone secured on the medallion. The medallion started to shake. The stone popped from the prongs that held it and it fell to the floor. The medallion knew. It did have the power he suspected. It would not let just any stone be placed on it. He had to have the real stones if he ever wanted the medallion to become as powerful as he knew it was. He needed the medallion in one piece for him to become King Texacia, the new King of all Mayans. He would become King if these two policemen would only do their jobs.

Miguel had his airplane put on constant readiness. He just needed to hear the word and he would be on his way.

"Mister Hernandos, I am checking in sir," Captain Sanchez said into his cell phone.

"Tell me some good news."

"My cousin Palo has gotten a job at the Inn. He will be on the inside. The men we are following are doing some repairs in the Inn. He will be able to overhear some of their conversation. It may help us find the stones you want," Sanchez said.

"That is good, but work faster. We need to conclude this assignment as soon as possible. If they hear about the Archeologist's death, they may panic and go to the police."

"Sir, if they do that they will go to prison for theft of a national treasure."

"I know that but they may cut a deal. They may know more than we realize. We don't know what the Archeologist told them. All we know is they were to meet at the Inn in Somerset."

"I want you to search their homes, their business, anyplace where they may have hidden those stones. As soon as they find out about the death of the Archeologist they will do something that may lose us the chance of ever getting the stones. That can't happen. They could destroy the stones if they think having them will send them to jail. Find those stones and find them quickly," Miguel said as he hung up the phone. Miguel was now seeing visions during the day. His mother was back again yelling at him to restore the family honor. Miguel didn't know what more he could do to get the stones back. He had to think through his splitting headache.

Sanchez had to act and had to do it quickly. He didn't want the wrath of Miguel to land on him. He would have to start searching for the stones immediately.

CHAPTER THIRTY-THREE

"Palo you have come at the right time. Two of my regular wait staff have quit. I didn't know what I was going to do. If you are half as good as you say you are we'll get along real well. There is only one more question. Why have you come to Somerset to work?"

Palo knew that question would be asked and he had come up with a lie that he thought would work.

"Some day I want to own my own place like this in Mexico. I can't get the experience in Mexico in how to deal with the American people. I have some friends that live in Pittsburgh and I was driving on the bus and saw this beautiful building. I found out it was a bed and breakfast and I knew this would be the place for me to learn about how the Americans like to be treated."

Jon was impressed at Palo's answer and decided to give him a chance.

CHAPTER THIRTY-FOUR

"Palo, you are doing an excellent job. Where did you pick up your skills as a waiter?" asked Jon.

"I worked in Cancun for a few years. My family is from that area," Palo said as he unloaded dishes from the serving tray.

"My friends who are doing the remodeling just came back from there. In fact, there is supposed to be someone coming from Cancun to stay for a few days. Maybe you know the man. He is an archeologist working on one of the Mayan ruins," Jon said.

"I know there are a number of people doing that down there. It seems to be of interest now. When he gets here, I will talk with him if it doesn't interfere with my work," Palo said.

"Palo, it is part of your job to make the guests feel comfortable. We want them to feel as if this home is their home while they are here. When you get your own place, you will need to make sure your guests feel comfortable when they are guests at your bed and breakfast."

Palo had finished cleaning and resetting the tables for the next meal. He started polishing the silverware as Jon was checking the liquor for re-supply of the bar stock.

"If you have time, Mister Jon, could you tell me who built such a beautiful home here in Somerset? The man must have been very wealthy," said Palo continuing to polish the silverware.

"This home was built in 1915 by a man whose name was Daniel Burnside Zimmerman. It took three years for the building to be completed. Mister Zimmerman was a coal and cattle baron. He owned a number of coal mines in the Somerset area and he also was involved in raising cattle in five or six states out west.

"How did he start becoming so rich?" asked Palo.

"Daniel Zimmerman's father was a farmer here in Somerset. One day Daniel read an article in a farm magazine about raising cattle in North Dakota. The grass was so rich in food value that the cattle grew fatter quicker. At the age of fourteen he went off to North Dakota to purchase his first cattle and start raising them on the rich Dakota grass. That was in 1877. By the time he was fifty, he was the largest independent cattle rancher in the country. He would send 40,000 cattle a year to market."

"Why did he build the house in Somerset?" asked Palo.

"Daniel was born in Somerset. He was a very smart businessman. He believed in the coal business as well as his cattle and he helped develop many coal towns in this area. He had interest in more than 140,000 acres of coal fields. He was the county's largest independent coal operator. He also owned a saw mill, a grist mill and many farms. He started many new improved farming techniques that made all the farms he owned profitable. But, I think I got off the subject a little, Palo. You asked why he built the house here. As you can see, the site stands high on this hill. He had a house in town and wanted a show place. He had the architect design a house with nine fireplaces. Four on the first floor one in the basement and four on the second floor. In the basement there are exceptionally high ceilings and there was a sleeping room designed for the man who tended the coal furnace. There was a potato cellar built beneath a brick courtyard, which is no longer here. The house had all the modern conveniences of its day. A central vacuuming system, an intercom system, and an air filtration system were built into the house. After ninety years you can still see evidences of a number of these conveniences still here.

Mister Zimmerman always wanted to do things right. He planted the trees and shrubs years before he decided to build the house on this property. Part of the land was made into a commercial apple orchard."

"Was the man who designed this house from Somerset?" asked Palo.

No. Mister Zimmerman found a well known architect of his day who had designed houses for some of his friends and asked him to design one for him.

The room on the third floor, the Trumbauer, is named after the famous Philadelphia architect, Horace Trumbauer who designed the house. Mister Zimmerman had Trumbauer build the house. It took three years to construct. During that time the family lived in their home in downtown Somerset. After everything was finalized and everything in the house was the way Mister Zimmerman wanted it, the family rode up the hill in their carriage one day and walked into the completed mansion. The trees were almost fully grown by then. Little of the mansion could be seen by those riding by on the road. His wife Lizzy, their two children, a daughter named Sally and a son named Ralph, lived here with him. When this house was built it was the only building at the top of this hill. The area looked very different than it does now. There was a building on the north side of the house for keeping horses in the early days, and automobiles later on. The front entrance of the property was at the bottom of the hill just off of the main road. In later years the house was fully concealed from everyone because the trees had grown so tall."

Jon stopped his history lesson to answer the ringing phone.

Palo was enjoying learning about the old home but he had to get word to Captain Sanchez. The Archeologist was expected any day. They would have to move fast to find the stones before the men started to suspect something had happened to their friend.

Sanchez sat in his rented car watching Bob and Mike unload the lumber. He needed to search their homes to see if he could find any signs of the stones. He had followed Bob the day before to know where he lived, and he also knew that Mike lived in an old house near Lake Somerset.

He headed first to Mike's house since it was the closest to the Inn. It seemed this home would be the easier of the two to break in. The house was old and the neighbors lived far enough away that someone could get close to the house without being noticed. Sanchez parked the rented Jeep a half-mile away from Mike's house and walked along the road then up the gravel driveway. He had purchased a gas can to use as an excuse if anyone stopped him. He was just a guy who had run out of gas and was hoping someone would be home to help him. He walked up the front steps of the house. After knocking for a minute He tried the door knob. The door was locked. He walked around to the back of the house. He knocked on the back door while testing to see if the door was unlocked. The door opened. He looked around to see if there was anyone watching. He stepped inside and closed the door. The door had opened onto a small porch. The porch was full of wood ready for the cold winters of Somerset. He tried the inner door and found it unlocked too. He carefully opened the inner door. He didn't know if there was anyone living in the house with Mike.

Sanchez stood in the kitchen for a minute after closing the door. He couldn't hear any signs of life. He started looking through everything in the kitchen. As a policeman in Mexico, he had searched many houses. He never made any attempt in the past to be gentle with the person's possessions he was searching, and he didn't know how to do that now. Sugar, salt, and napkins were thrown on the floor as he looked under and around everything he could. The more he looked the more frustrated he became. There was a suitcase lying on the floor of the bedroom. He took his knife and ripped out the lining hoping the stones were hidden there. He checked under the mattress and behind every drawer. He found nothing. He had been in the house for an hour and thought he had better leave. He returned to his car and drove back to the Inn to see if he could find the two men he was watching. *The other man Bob must have the stones,* he thought as he sat in his Jeep watching the now empty truck parked next to the Inn.

CHAPTER THIRTY-FIVE

Miguel could no longer stay in his treasure room knowing there was a missing piece to his life. Somewhere in the state of Pennsylvania, there were the Mayan stones that would make him the King of all the Mayans. His head spun with the thought of the greatness the stones possessed. Over the past few days Miguel had a difficult time keeping his mind on his business. He was a person who liked running everything on his own. The business had gotten so big that Miguel had his cousin Carlos become a partner. He had let Carlos run the illegal aspects of his operation.

Getting out of drug distribution and stolen property had made Miguel almost a legitimate businessman. Miguel had known that going into legal businesses was the way to go to assure a strong future. He had always been drawn to the tough life of his past. Carlos, with his Masters Degree in Business, had moved Miguel's money into arenas that Miguel had never found to be comfortable. By being a legitimate business man, however, it gave Miguel the opportunity to discover new ways to gain additional Mayan treasures. He was now on the National Board of Antiquities. He knew all of the sources of new Mayan treasures legal and otherwise.

All people interested in the Mayan culture and those who wanted to explore any of the thousands of sites, needed to get permission from the National Board of Antiquities. This gave Miguel first crack at where the new treasures were. If there was a new piece that Miguel wanted, he could trace its location and either buy it or steal it.

Miguel had traveled over many parts of South America to fund the discovery of Mayan artifacts. Today all the treasures he had seen did not compare to the ones now located in a little hamlet in Pennsylvania, United States. Miguel became deep in thought about the feeling he received when he put on the medallion for the first time. He had put on the medallion many times since, but nothing ever happened again. No feelings came as they did the first time. He wanted to try again to see if something would happen.

With the new full moon shining through his window, Miguel took the medallion from his personal safe and put it over his head. As the necklace fell in place around his neck, flashes of light came into Miguel's mind. The flashes blinded his eyes. He heard hundreds of voices screaming in pain. He felt as though he had entered hell. He didn't have the strength to tear the medallion from his neck. His head was spinning. He felt as if he were going to be sick from spinning round and round. He wanted to fall to the floor but couldn't. As he felt ready to collapse and give up the struggle against the power of the necklace, the spinning stopped. He felt as though he was standing on the edge of a precipice. His toes were over the edge and he could, at any second, fall into the abyss. He heard a voice from somewhere above him. It was a deep man's voice calling out his name, "Miguel, Miguel Hernandos," the deep voice chanted.

Miguel had been struck dumb. His feet felt as if they were going to slip off the edge and he had no control to stop it.

"Miguel, Miguel Hernandos," the deep voice chanted again.

This time Miguel pulled his courage together and weakly called out.

"I am here. I don't want to die. I want to live," he cried out.

"Miguel you are not going to die. You are going to serve your ancestors. You are the one chosen to bring back our glory days. We are the rightful heirs to all the land for 1,000 miles in every direction from where you stand. We have been stripped of our wealth by the Europeans who came with their guns and their sickness to take our country from us. You are the one who will bring back our power and our glory." the voice told him.

"What am I to do?" Miguel asked feeling an inner strength seeping into his body.

"You are to unite the holy stones to the medallion you now wear around your neck. You will go now and find a way to make it happen before the next full moon. You will bring the necklace back to the tomb of the Child King. You will watch the power of the necklace as it destroys all who do not believe. You have tasted the beginning of the power at this full moon. The storms that raked the ancient city of Tiaka have allowed the necklace to be found, but a non-believer found a way to steal the medallion's power. The desecration of the necklace is why you were told to kill the man who did this," the voice told him.

"You were the one in my head who told me to put the pillow over the Archeologist's head?" Miguel asked.

"Yes it was I. There will be others who you will have to be eliminated before we will again gain our rightful place in Mayan history."

"What do you want me to do?" Miguel asked the voice.

"Go as quickly as you can. We will guide you. Take the necklace and replace the stones. You will then have the power to do all that is needed to bring back the glory of our people. Remember all the stones must be put back into the necklace before the power will be restored. You must be on your guard for those who will try to fool you in your quest. You will not lose if you heed my warning. Go and you will soon be our King."

Miguel suddenly came out of his trance and was standing in the same spot he was when he put the necklace around his neck.

The clock chimed six times. He had been standing in the same place for six hours. He collapsed on the floor. He now knew what he had to do and how he was going to do it.

CHAPTER THIRTY-SIX

"Sir, the Chancellor of Pennsylvania State University is on the phone," the secretary to the President of Mexico said.

"What could he want?" asked the President.

"He says he met you last year at a conference of colleges held in San Diego, California. He wants to talk to you about one of their professors."

The President of Mexico walked to the phone recalling the conference held by the International Organization of Colleges in San Diego last year. He had met many wonderful people from the United States. He remembered one man in particular, Mario Martella, from Penn State University. They had many of the same interests one of which was the Mayan civilization. Both men came to find out they had been part of the same archeological dig in Columbia. They had enjoyed a few pleasant hours over dinner talking about their experiences at the dig and reminiscing over the joys of being part of digging up a lost civilization.

"Mario, how nice it is to talk to you again. How is your lovely wife Eleanora?" asked the President of Mexico.

"Thank you for asking, my wife and I are doing very well. Mister President, I know you are very busy and I hate to have to call you, but I don't know the proper channels to go through for this sort of thing." the Chancellor said.

"What is it?" asked the Mexican President anxiously.

"Our University has had, for the past few years, a man doing some archeological work on a Mayan ruin north of Cancun. We received all the approvals from the Board of Antiquities. We expected most of the relics he found would stay in your country. Our man found out someone was taking most of the important finds and selling them to a person somewhere near Mexico City. I have just been told by one of his colleagues that he has been killed."

"That is terrible. Was it an accident of some sort? What was the man's name?" asked the President.

"No sir, we think it was murder. The name of the Archeologist was Andrew Kosco. One of his colleagues received a phone call saying Andrew was shot and was in a coma. When he asked how it happened he wasn't given an answer. He went down to Mexico to find out what happened. Our man questioned some of the workers at the dig site and was told Andrew was shot by a local policeman. The policeman tried to tell the men working at the dig site it was self defense. He said that Andrew attacked the policeman after he was told that a necklace Andrew found was to be sent to the Museum in Mexico City."

"Isn't it normal procedure for the items to go to the Museum?" asked the President.

"Yes sir, but Andrew thought it was odd he was never told who had the treasures. A few times he wanted to restudy the pieces he had found, however, he was told by the policeman who had taken them they were locked away and he couldn't see them. Andrew put a GPS computer chip in an urn. He traced the urn to a private residence near Mexico City. The man's name is Miguel Hernandos. We found out that Miguel and the policeman were the last to see Andrew alive. After they left the hospital room, the nurse went in and found him dead."

"Is there any proof they did it? If there is I will have them arrested immediately," the President said.

"No sir, but what is odd is that the body is to be cremated and the ashes are to be sent back to the United States. This is very unusual. The only approval that the clinic had to get for the body to be cremated was from the police Captain. There was no reason given for the cremation. It is very suspicious."

"What do you want me to do?" asked the President.

"Could you find a way to see if this man, Miguel Hernandos, is stealing artifacts? Maybe there also needs to be an inquiry into the actions of the police Captain who is supposedly trafficking in Mayan treasures," the Chancellor said.

"I will have someone on it today. I am sorry for your loss. I hope this doesn't destroy any future interactions between your University and our country," said the President.

"Thank you for your time Mister President. I hope we get some answers. We have worked too hard to have anything like this ruin our relationship. Thank you again," the Chancellor said and hung up.

CHAPTER THIRTY-SEVEN

"Sam, I've been robbed. My house has been turned upside down," yelled Bob into the phone.

"Are you alright?" Sam asked.

"I'm fine but someone has pulled everything in the place apart."

"What did they take?" asked Sam.

"Well nothing that I can tell so far."

"Did they take the computer, your TV, or any of your electronics?" Sam asked.

"Well, let me see," Bill said looking around at the mess.

"No, all that stuff is here and on the floor. It looks like someone came in here and just trashed everything."

"Shit!" Sam exclaimed, "Do you think someone was looking for the gems?"

"Maybe you're right. But whoever did this must have gotten pretty mad at not finding them. Do you think it's someone from the police department in Cancun?" he questioned.

"We can't jump to that conclusion yet. It could have been just some kids getting their kicks trashing your place."

"I don't think so. I just checked the refrigerator and the liquor cabinet and everything is still there. Some bottles of liquor are broken but none were taken. Should I report this to the police?" he asked.

"I think we better wait on that. They will come up with the same conclusion about it being kids and they will start asking more questions than we have answers for at this time. Can you get things back in order?" Sam asked.

"It will take me all night. I'll call Mike and have him come over and help."

"I'll be over in a little while. This flu has just about run its course and I'm feeling a lot better. We can think this through as we put you back together."

"What are you going to do with the three necklaces? Are they in a safe place?" asked Bob.

"I'll bring them with me. Let me call Mike and you can start cleaning up," Sam said hanging up the phone.

Sam was starting to get very worried. They should never have gotten involved with this Archeologist. It was the dumbest thing Mike and Bob had ever gotten into. *The damage was done now,* Sam thought. *We will have to get a hold of this Andrew guy, and give him the gems and wash our hands of the whole thing before we all end up in jail or in worse shape.*

CHAPTER THIRTY-EIGHT

"This is the President's office calling. I want to talk to the person in charge."

"The Director is out of the office at the moment. Could you tell me the President of what?" asked the nurse in charge.

"The President of Mexico, Carlos Diaz," was the reply.

The nurse sat up and almost dropped the phone. I'm sorry. I didn't expect to be getting a call from the President. What can I do for you?"

I need to talk with the person in charge about the American who died in your clinic."

"What do you need to know?" the nurse asked.

"Is the body still there?"

"We have just sent the body to be cremated, as requested by Captain Sanchez, of the local police department."

"Get that body back. I want to have a full autopsy. I want to know for certain how the man died."

"He was brought in here with a gunshot wound. We thought he had a good chance to make a recovery, but he died. We thought he died from the gunshot. There didn't seem to be any reason to spend the little money we have for an autopsy on a man who had been shot."

"Didn't it seem odd that the body was to be cremated? The normal procedure is to send the body to the country of the deceased's origin," the president's aide said.

"That is true, but Captain Sanchez was concerned with the possibility of disease and signed the order. We thought it was unusual, but with the signed order we followed all the needed regulations."

"Call now and stop the cremation. I hope it's not too late," yelled the president's aide into the phone.

CHAPTER THIRTY-NINE

I must follow my orders from the voice in my vision. I must go to the United States and be there when the stones are found. No one knows me there and I can come up with a good reason for being in Somerset, Pennsylvania.

Miguel thought about a reason for being in the Somerset area for a few minutes. He had a computer hook-up to the websites in the United States, through a satellite connection. He needed information about this place called the Inn at Somerset. He found the web site for The Inn and enjoyed reading about the mansion.

He carefully typed the web address and was connected to the web page. He picked up his cell phone and called.

"The Inn, how may I help you?" said Jon, the Inn Keeper.

"I need a room for a few days. This is Miguel Hernandos from Mexico."

"Yes sir. We don't often get calls from Mexico for our rooms. How did you find out about us?" asked Jon.

"I am on your web site and from the looks of your beautiful building; it would suit my needs perfectly. I will be coming up to have some trade talks with people from Pittsburgh. I am looking to open a business in the area and want to experience the American Bed and Breakfast. I have never been to one." Miguel said in his most pleasant voice.

"When do you want to stay?" asked Jon.

"I would like your best, most expensive room, and I will need it for five days starting tonight."

"I have someone staying in the Library Suite, which is our nicest room. I do have the Hillside Manor Suite. I'm sure you will be comfortable in it, or I'm sure you would like the D.B. Zimmerman or the Sally Zimmerman rooms."

"Can you move the people out of the Library Suite? I will pay for their room and meals for the length of their stay," Miguel said.

"One moment. The person who is renting the room is sitting here next to me," Jon said.

Through his muffled voice Miguel could hear Jon ask through the phone, "Queen Susan, someone wants to rent your room and will pay for your stay and your meals. Do you want to switch to the Hillside Manor?"

Miguel could hear this person called Queen Susan answer, "Who is he?"

"He is from Mexico and he wants to open up a business in the area." After a minute, Jon came back on the phone, "Mister Hernandos the room is yours," Jon said.

"Did I overhear you call her Queen? From what country is she from?" Miguel asked inquisitively. Jon laughed. She is the honorary Queen of the Inn. I am sure the two of you will get along very well. She will provide you with lots of stories about the Inn. May I have a credit card number to secure the room?"

Miguel couldn't be happier. He had his plan set and the next few days would be the turning point in his life he could feel it.

CHAPTER FORTY

"Thanks, you two, for helping straighten up this place. We still haven't come up with a solution to these gems we have. I wish we would hear from Andrew," Bob said as he pulled three beers out of the refrigerator.

The three sat in the kitchen drinking a beer. It was three o'clock in the morning. They were all exhausted. They managed to get most of the house back in order.

"Do you think this mess was caused by someone looking for the gems?" asked Mike.

"I'm sure of it. I would like to know who and how they tracked us back home," Sam said.

"The only person we talked to in Cancun was Andrew. I'll bet the police were following him and when they saw him talking with Bob and me in the bar, they followed us. Shit. We are in deep trouble now just like you said we would be Sam," Mike said.

"Let's not get into that now. We need to find out where Andrew is and get rid of these gems. If we don't hear from him in a day or two we should bury them or better yet, give them to the police and tell them the whole story," Bob said.

"We need a lawyer first. Maybe we can get off with a slap on the wrist," Sam replied.

They all sat quietly for the next few minutes and drank their beer.

"Did Andrew mention anything else that you can remember? Some way to contact him?" asked Sam.

Mike started looking through his wallet.

"What are you looking for?" asked Sam.

"For some reason I think Andrew gave me a piece of paper. I'm trying to find it. Here it is: Doctor Andrew Kosco, Archeologist, Pennsylvania State University, State College, Pennsylvania. His cell phone is on this paper too."

"Why in the hell have you been keeping that a secret?" asked Bob.

"No one asked. I was expecting to see him any day. I didn't think we would need it until Sam asked," Mike replied.

"Let's call him now and find out when he is going to be here," said Sam

"It's almost four o'clock in the morning," said Mike.

"Who the hell cares? We are the ones the police are after. I don't give a shit if I wake him up." said Bob.

Mike dialed the phone number. The phone rang six times before someone picked it up.

"*Sí*," the voice said sleepily.

"Is this the number to reach Andrew Kosco, the Archeologist?" Mike said.

The voice hesitated.

"Hello, are you there?" asked Mike.

"*Sí Señor*. This was the phone for Mister Andrew," the voice said.

"Where is he?" asked Mike.

"He is dead, *Señor*," the voice said and the phone went dead.

Mike tried to call the number back but the connection could not be made. The person on the other end must have disabled the phone.

"What?" asked Bob.

Mike stood there for a few seconds to catch his breath from what he had just heard. It was difficult for his brain to believe what the man on the other end of the phone had said.

"A man answered and said Andrew is dead. He then hung up the phone and must have disconnected it in some way. I can't get him back," Mike said as he stood in the kitchen just staring at the floor.

CHAPTER FORTY-ONE

Miguel first noticed the building as the car rounded the turn on the interstate highway from Pittsburgh. Miguel was enchanted by the old house from a distance. As the Rolls Royce left the interstate and turned the corner at the bottom of the hill, the Georgian style architectural seemed pleasant to his eye. He was used to the one-story Mexican stucco homes built for the many hot days. Here in the North the weather was much more severe. Homes needed to be built to withstand the wind, rain and cold. *A home like this,* he thought, *was built to last. The home was already ninety years old and looked to be standing the test of time rather well.* As the car started up the hill toward the Inn, Miguel's eyes followed the lines of the building from top to bottom. Coming up the hill he could see the four large chimneys. A slate roof pierced by five dormers topped the building with grace. Balanced well on the second floor were seven windows across the front of the building. The white keystones above each window sparkled in the sunshine. The first floor porch stood majestically on four white marble columns in the middle and two sturdy brick end supports. An iron railing surrounded the porch roof. Wings on each side of the structure balanced well with the main building. On the right side of the house was an enclosed sun room and to the left a two story wing was set back from the main entrance. The front entrance door was complemented by oval windows on each side accenting the grandeur of the wide entrance door. As the chauffeur parked, Miguel thought the house invited him to enter. It was big and he thought it could be overpowering to some, but the grace of the building invited any weary traveler for a night's respite. Miguel couldn't be more pleased with the chance to spend some time here. He knew he had come here for a reason greater than the mere comforts of a few nights stay, but to find such a gracious place made the adventure even more fulfilling. As he waited for his chauffeur to open his door, a man came out the front entrance. He was obviously Jon, the innkeeper. Miguel knew he was going to enjoy his stay, especially after he recovered the stones that rightly belonged to him.

"Welcome. You must be Mister Hernandos," Jon said greeting Miguel as he exited his limousine. Jon was looking at a Rolls Royce, Silver Cloud parked across five parking spaces in front of the Inn. Although there was a man in Somerset, who owned one of the fine cars, it was the only time he had ever seen one painted fire engine red. Jon walked to the open trunk and started to take one of the bags.

"Do not bother. My chauffer will take care of them."

The chauffeur carried in the bags and stood waiting for instructions. The driver looked his part. He had a chauffeur's cap and a three-piece white suit with a great coat to match.

"I thought you flew in from Mexico." Jon said as he found the key to the Library Suite.

"I did, but I can't seem to leave my toy behind. Since it fit in the plane, I have brought it along. I thought it would impress the men I am to meet.

"Will you need a room for your chauffer and your pilot?" Jon asked.

"No, Captain Michael and my chauffer will be staying elsewhere. It seems my chauffer has some cousins who live in Pittsburgh and Captain Michael is going to visit his brother. They will spend tonight and tomorrow with them. If I need to get around the town, is there a place I can buy a car?"

"Buy a car?" asked Jon.

"Yes. I don't like to rent those dirty things. I'll buy one and give it to my chauffeur's cousin when I am finished with it," Miguel said as they walked in the front door.

"How very generous of you. Is there any room in your family for an inn keeper?" Jon said laughingly.

It took a minute for Miguel to get the humor in the remark, but then he burst out laughing.

"I came from a poor family. Through the early years of my life I had to rely on the generosity of many family members. Now that I have, how you Americans say, made it, I feel it is my turn to give back as often as I can," Miguel said.

"You are truly a unique person," Jon said as he showed Miguel up the stairs to the Library Suite. The chauffeur followed the two men.

"I hope you enjoy your stay here," Jon said.

"I have already enjoyed the drive from Pittsburgh. The view of the building from the highway is impressive. The building is so different from those in my country.

CHAPTER FORTY-TWO

"These bastards are driving me crazy. I need to get these stones and get out of this freezing place," Sanchez said to himself.

Sanchez had ripped apart the house Mike lived in to no avail. There was no sign of the jewels. He was already tired of the cold weather. His hands and feet were cold from the time he landed at the airport. He wanted to get back to the warmth of Mexico. He was not only cold, he was hungry. The shit these people ate was making his stomach ache. He needed some good Mexican food. He needed food that was hot and spicy. This American food was killing his stomach. There is one real Mexican restaurant in Somerset but it is closed for vacation. He wanted to find the jewels and head for home as soon as he could. He was now sitting in his rented Jeep outside Bob's home with the car's heater at full blast. The house was further out in the country than Mike's. There were a couple of barns on the property filled with horses, cows, and llamas. Sanchez carefully looked through all the buildings over the last hour. He wanted to be sure he knew everything he could about the man he was following. The other man, Mike, lived in a home probably owned by his family. This place was very different. This was a person who loved animals and would rather be with his animals than people. The barns were sparkling clean. The animals were cared for better than most of the people in

Mexico. Sanchez was sure the stones were hidden somewhere on this property. Sanchez was sure Bob would keep them close to a location he could easily get to in case he had to move them. Sanchez decided he would search the barn first and then, if necessary, he would move in and search the house.

He now had spent half the night ransacking the barns. He had kept in close contact with his cousin Palo to make sure he knew where Bob was at all times. Palo was trying to work his job at the Inn and help follow Bob and Mike. He was now sitting in his rented car outside the home of Mike. There were two additional cars in the driveway. Palo was dead tired. He had worked all day serving a group of fifty-two people on a bus tour that included lunch at the Inn. He enjoyed the new job and the people he worked with. His problem was the night work for his cousin Sanchez. He needed to get some rest, but he never had the time for that. As his eyes were closing and slumber was overtaking him, the cell phones shrill jostled him awake.

"*Sí,*" he said as best he could.

"Were you sleeping? You will have enough time to sleep when you are dead. Now I expect you to be awake and doing what I ask. Understood?" Sanchez yelled into the phone.

"Yes cousin. What do you want?"

"Where are the two?" he asked.

"There are three, not two. Did you ever think there were more than two since the name of their company was the Three Studs?" asked Palo.

Sanchez was not the smartest chili in the basket. He didn't think that the Three Studs Construction Company meant that there were three people involved in the Company. It just didn't dawn on him. He could kick himself for being so stupid, but others have been kicking him for years for his stupidity. He didn't need to kick himself.

"Where are the three of them?" Sanchez asked into the cell phone.

"They have been at the house all night cleaning up the mess you made during your search."

"I have been searching the property of the man named Bob. I am going into the house to find the stones. Call me if any of them leave."

Sanchez didn't have to try to sneak into the house. He knew there was no one there. He had watched the house in between searching the barns. He didn't see any lights in the house all night. He entered through the back screened porch. The people who live in the United States were very trusting. All the back doors seem to be unlocked. Sanchez searched as he did before, with no care for the possessions of the owner of the place. When he was done, he was totally frustrated. He didn't find any indication of any stones at all. In his frustration he stood in the middle of the living room and lit a Mexican cigar. The pungent smelling smoke wafted up and filled the place. Sanchez stood in the middle of the room and tried to think where else the man could have hidden the stones. He finished the cigar without any new ideas on where to look. He dropped the cigar onto the carpet and crushed it with his boot. The old carpet smoldered from the hot ash. Sanchez didn't pay any attention to the smoke starting to billow from the carpet. He moved back into the kitchen and again looked through the closets and the refrigerator. He had run out of ideas where to look. He glanced into the living room and saw smoke rising from the carpet. He moved into the room to see what was burning. As he entered the room, a whoosh of flames sprang up from a wicker basket. Before Sanchez could respond, the flames started leaping from item to item throughout the room. Sanchez moved to the back door and quickly disappeared into the night. He had to get away before someone saw the flames and saw him fleeing the scene.

The old farmhouse was a tinderbox. The flames started to lick the curtains in the living room. Flames spread rapidly through the entire first floor. In a matter of minutes the flames had eaten through the ceiling into the upstairs bedrooms. A window in the living room finally blew out from the heat. Now that the fire had a vent, the flames shot out the window and licked their way up the side of the building to the roof.

A neighbor a half mile away, making coffee at his usual time of 3:45 a.m., saw the flames as they burst through the roof of the house. He quickly called 911 and hurriedly put his clothes on to see if he could be of any help to his neighbor. The car that was driving away from the fire wasn't noticed by anyone.

Sanchez needed to get some sleep. He had had a busy night.

CHAPTER FORTY-THREE

The three were about ready to collapse from exhaustion. It was four a.m. and they now knew Andrew would never be coming to get them off the hook with the gems.

"Now what are we suppose to do?" asked Mike.

"I sure as hell don't know," Bob said.

"Great. The two brain trusts that got us into this mess are at a loss as to how to get us out of it. Why don't we take the gems to the police tomorrow and throw ourselves on the mercy of the court? We could plead absolute stupidity. That would be the truth. Hell, we probably will be the ones accused of killing Andrew. He was the one that found the gems and we are the ones that have them, ergo guilty!" yelled Sam.

"You make it sound like we are up shit's creek without a paddle," Mike said.

"That's exactly what I'm saying. The guys that are now following us are probably the ones who killed Andrew. They don't seem the type that would let any of us stand in their way of getting the gems." Sam said.

As the three stood in the kitchen the phone rang. None of them wanted to answer it. No good news ever came at four in the morning.

"Hello," Mike said.

"Mike its Charles Stone, is your brother with you, I hope?"

"It's for you. It's Charles Stone."

"Yeah, Charles, what's up? No shit. I'm on my way," Bob said as he put down the phone and reached for his jacket.

"What's the problem?" asked Sam.

"My house is on fire. The fire department is on the way but Charles said he could see it from his place and it doesn't look good. He was hoping I wasn't part of the blaze. I have to get back. I have to try to save the animals."

"We'll go with you," Bob said as they all got their coats on and headed for the truck.

More exhausted than the three thought they could possibly be, they led the last of the animals out of the barns just as a precaution. The barns had not been damaged but Bob didn't want to take any chances that some of the sparks might ignite the old wooden buildings. If that happened they would never have enough time to get the animals to safety. The three stood looking at the fire finally being doused by the fire truck. The sun had come up and the area was a black sooty mess on top of what remained of the white snow. Their noses and ears were red and their faces were blackened with smoke.

The fire trucks were wrapping up their gear and the three had gotten the animals back in the barns. The three stood looking at the remains of the farm house. They knew they had to get some rest.

"I would have you'd two come to my place but I only have one bed. You are welcome to sleep on the floor if you like," Sam said.

"We'll crash at Mike's for a few hours. I need a shower, some sleep and Mike has some of my clothes that I have left at his place," Bob said.

"Why don't we meet at the Inn for an early dinner at about five o'clock tonight? We can figure out what to do then. I don't want to be carrying all three necklaces with the gems. How about we each take one, that way whoever wants them will have to kill all three of us," Sam said. The other two reluctantly each took a necklace and stuffed it into their pocket.

"Watch your back Sam," Bob said as he dropped Sam off.

"You two do the same. See you tonight."

CHAPTER FORTY-FOUR

"I was told to call this number if I had any news about the American that died here in Cancun," the nurse said.

"If you will give me the information I will pass it on."

"How can I be sure that the President will get the information? When he called he wanted to get the information personally," the nurse said.

"The President is my husband. He is in the shower at the moment. Do you want to wait for him to come to the phone?"

"No. I'm sorry for calling at an inappropriate time," the nurse said.

"What is the information you have for him," the President's wife asked.

"The American, Andrew Kosco, died of suffocation. When we realized this we checked the extra pillow that was in his room. There were traces of his saliva found on the pillow."

"Do you have any idea who might have done this?" she asked.

"The only people who were in the room were; doctors, nurses, the police Captain, and his friend."

"Do you know the police Captain and his friend's name?" she asked.

Captain Sanchez and Miguel Hernandos," the nurse said.

"I will inform the President. If he has any more questions, what is your number where he can reach you in the next ten minutes?" The nurse gave the information and hung up.

As the President stood in front of his dressing room mirror checking some new gray hairs, and a few extra pounds that seemed to appear overnight, his wife entered.

"It would be better if you had a smaller mirror," she said.

"Why?" he asked.

"The added pounds don't fit in a smaller mirror my dear," she said laughingly.

"I heard the phone ring. Anything I should know about?" he asked.

She relayed the phone message from the clinic.

The President immediately made a call.

"I have just heard your professor was murdered. Someone used a pillow to keep him from continuing his work. Someone wants to keep a very big secret. I will do whatever I can to clear this up. What can I do for you at this time?"

The President listened for a moment and said, "I will make sure they will be given any help they need to solve this mystery. I want you to understand, anything found on Mexican soil is the property of the country, until it is officially released. We continue to have very liberal policies regarding artifacts on tour, so we surely can come up with an equitable arrangement for anything found. I hope I am making sense my friend," the President said to the Chancellor of Pennsylvania State University.

"Thank you Mister President. I will be having two of our men at the dig site in a matter of hours. I will let you know what leads they may be able to uncover. I will keep you informed."

CHAPTER FORTY-FIVE

"Jon, I need a room for a couple of days until I figure out what I'm going to do. Mike and I get along but I need a little more privacy and staying here will have me close to work," Bob said as he stood at the check-in counter.

"We have space. I'll put you on the third floor in the Garret. It should do nicely."

"I don't have any luggage since everything was burned up in the fire," Bob said.

"I'm sorry to hear about the fire. Have they figured out how it started?" asked Jon.

"Not yet. They should be able to tell me more tomorrow. I need to go up the street and get some clothes. With the snow we are expecting, I think I'll need something more than what I have on," Bob said, leaving to get some warm winter clothes.

"Excuse me, Jon, did I hear you say it was going to snow tonight?" asked Miguel as he sat in the living room near the roaring fire.

"We are supposed to get three to five inches tonight. It will be just enough to make it difficult getting around."

"I have never seen snow falling. There are traces of it on the ground now and it's the first I have seen in a very long time, but I have never seen it falling from the sky. Does it fall as quickly as rain?" Miguel asked gleefully.

"I think you should see it for yourself. Explaining it doesn't do it justice," Jon said as he left the room to attend to an incoming guest for dinner.

CHAPTER FORTY-SIX

"Mister Chancellor, we wanted you to know as soon as we found out anything," the Professor said from Andrew's dig site.

"Go ahead. I want to know all the details. Leave nothing out," the Chancellor said.

The two men told him about getting to the dig site with Andrew's man Raul. Raul had shown them where they were digging and the episode of Andrew coming over the hill with the necklace and medallion. The two men traced the steps of Andrew and found the entrance Andrew fell into. They used a rope to get into the burial chamber and found the coffin Andrew must have found. They too managed to get the top off and saw Andrew's flashlight and the mummy without the necklace. Their knowledge of the writings soon told them of the jewels that were encrusted on the medallion that should have been around the mummy's neck. Their knowledge of the Mayan civilization told them this was a major find and the gems would be worth millions on the open market. They would be priceless in historical value. When they relayed this information to the Chancellor, he immediately conferred with the President of Mexico.

"Mister President, we have a situation most important to both our countries."

The Chancellor relayed all the information he had been told.

"What do you think we should do about this?" asked the President of Mexico.

"The fewer people who know about this the better. I think we have some innocent people and some serious criminals involved in this. I don't want any international incident over this. Nothing good will come of it. If the newspapers or television reporters find out about this, we will both be boiled in oil. Let me locate the people who may be involved and see if we can find those who may have already killed for these gems. Does this sound like a workable plan?" asked the Chancellor.

"I will be here waiting to hear from you. Being boiled in oil can wait for a while. I will expect a call whenever you hear anything. I am at a state dinner tonight but I can be reached at any time. Call the number you currently have. I will be waiting to hear from you. Good luck," the President said and hung up.

The Chancellor hung up the phone and quickly redialed.

"This is the Chancellor. I want the head of the campus police in my office sooner than ASAP. I have a job more important than any he has ever had," the Chancellor said and hung up. He sat at his desk, steepled his fingers and thought about how he was going to keep this from becoming an international incident.

CHAPTER FORTY-SEVEN

"Sanchez, this is Miguel."

"Where are you? You sound very close," Sanchez said into his cell phone.

"I am in the Inn."

"I thought you were going to stay in Mexico until I called you?"

"I couldn't wait and besides the *gringos* don't know who I am. What have you found out since I last talked with you?" asked Miguel.

"I have searched the house of the man named Bob," Sanchez said.

"I know, and it burned to the ground," replied Miguel.

"Things got out of hand. I tried to put out the flame but the fire spread too quickly."

"They surely know we are on to them by this time," said Miguel.

"The *gringos* are going to be at the Inn tonight. Palo overheard the Inn Keeper talking about them meeting for dinner. Maybe, since you are staying in the Inn, you could get close enough to them tonight to overhear where they have hidden the gems," Sanchez said.

"It seems I am the only one that has a chance of finding the gems. I will find out where they have hidden them and I will call you to go get them. We will then return to Mexico as soon as we find them," said Miguel.

"That will not be soon enough for me. The food here is not good and I am freezing all the time," Sanchez said with teeth chattering.

"I don't know, I am looking forward to seeing it snow tonight." Miguel said.

CHAPTER FORTY-EIGHT

"I wish we had built this bar for you. Why didn't you call us?" asked Mike as he entered the new bar at the Inn.

"I did, but you guys were so busy with those Pharmacy renovations that you were building, you didn't have time for my bar. How do you like it?" asked Jon.

"It's nice. The walnut fits in nicely with the rest of the room. This is a great addition to the place. Sam gave you an estimate?" asked Bob.

It was a good price but I wanted it sooner than you could deliver," said Jon,

"Oh yeah, that's right. Sam does all that figuring. We just do the grunt work," Mike said.

"I wish you did a little more grunting. I always seem to get the heavy end of all the jobs," Bob said as he grabbed a seat at the bar. There were only two seats left.

"Where is Sam going to sit?" Bob asked.

"Sam will have to stand. That skinny ass could just slide between our two seats," Mike said.

"Are you trying to tell me I got a big ass?" Bob said.

"I'm glad Jon ordered extra wide seats. That's all I have to say," Mike exclaimed.

The two of them continued to banter back and forth. They

each ordered a beer and waited for Sam. They sat nervously and fumbled with the necklace each had in their pocket. They both felt very uncomfortable having the gems that the men from Mexico seemed to be after. Both of them, if they would have known, would have thrown the gems away rather than go through what they already have had to put up with.

"How's your room?" asked Mike looking at the bubbles rising in his beer glass.

"Nice, it's a little too flowery for my taste, but the room is nice."

"Your taste is more toward deer skin pelts hanging on the walls," Mike said laughingly.

"Right. What would you know about decorating? The old homestead is exactly as Mom decorated it fifty years ago."

"I just liked the way she did it. I found no reason to change anything," Mike retorted.

"I could hear the two of you all the way at the bottom of the hill. There are other guests in here. They don't want to hear a couple of locals running their mouths," Sam said entering the bar.

Miguel was sitting in the corner of the bar having a glass of wine, and looking through a local newspaper. As Miguel concentrated on listening to the conversation of the two men sitting at the bar he almost dropped his wine glass when he heard the bartender say,

"Well, well here are The Three Studs back from their trip to Cancun. What dumb ass thing did you do this year that will get into the newspaper?" asked the bartender.

"It was a mistake and we didn't get kicked out of Aruba last year either," said Mike.

"How was the trip? Did you see lots of little bikinis?" asked the bartender.

"Bikinis are supposed to be little. That's what the word means: little swimsuit. And give me a beer. I'll be right back I need to pee," Sam said to the bartender.

The bartender set Sam's beer down and went into the back room to get a food order for one of the men sitting at the bar.

"Why don't we give these necklaces to Sam so we can stop worrying about them," Mike whispered to Bob.

"Quiet. Someone will hear you," Bob whispered back.

It was too late for Bob to tell Mike not to say anything about the necklaces. Miguel overheard their conversation. He had to get back to his room and call Sanchez. He now knew where the stones were. He should have lowered the newspaper to see what the other stud looked like. I'll see him after I get a hold of Sanchez. He now had to find a way to get the gems and get out of the country without anyone knowing it. Miguel left money and headed for his room to make the call.

"Is that true what you said to the bartender about bikinis?" Mike asked after Sam returned from the pee break.

"I don't know, but it sounded good," Sam said, taking a long drink from the bottle.

Miguel went to his room at the top of the stairs.

"Captain, did you know that a person named Sam is the third member of this group called The Three Studs?" asked Miguel

"It makes sense there are three but I didn't know the name was Sam. I only saw two men in the bar with the Archeologist. When they were on the beach there were only two men. Maybe the third one never went to Cancun," Sanchez said.

"We don't know that. We have to assume there were three studs and you screwed up. This third one named Sam seems to be smarter than the other two. Sam does the bookkeeping and may be the one with enough brains to have the stones. Find out where this third stud lives and check out his place," Miguel said and hung up.

When Miguel got back to his seat in the bar The Three Studs were gone. He ordered another glass of wine. He soon heard their voices coming from the dining room. Miguel noticed that Palo was serving dinner tonight. Miguel wrote a note in Spanish. He called Palo over as he passed his table in the bar.

"Excuse me, may I have a menu to look at for a minute?" asked Miguel.

Quickly looking over the menu Miguel asked Palo, "Before you go, this item here," Miguel asked as he pointed to the note tucked into the menu. Palo read and nodded his head.

"That is very good tonight. The sea bass is fresh and the lemon garlic butter brings out its flavor."

"Thank you for your help," Miguel said and ripped up the note in the menu. He handed the menu back to Palo. Palo took the menu and headed for the kitchen. Miguel had written on the note for Palo to listen to The Three Stud's conversation and report back to him.

CHAPTER FORTY-NINE

Sanchez was always a good policeman. He knew his job and he knew how to track those he needed to catch. The tracking of the men in Somerset, Pennsylvania, was very different, but very easy. None of them knew they were being followed. It was too bad he didn't know there were three instead of two people involved. He felt foolish for not thinking there might be more than two. Now that he knew there were three, he would just add one more to his list to watch. They each went about their business and within a day Sanchez knew where each of them lived, where their office was, if they were married or had girlfriends, (which they didn't) or if they had any pets living in their respective houses. Only one had a pet. Sam had a cat. He had successfully checked Mike's and Bob's houses along with their office. They had no safe in which to hide the stones and every conceivable place he could think of had been checked. The last house was Sam's. He hoped the stones were there.

Sanchez knew Sam was at the Inn working on the renovations. The double-wide trailer Sam lived in wouldn't take long. This time he had to be more discreet. Miguel became very upset when he heard Bob's farmhouse had burned to the ground.

"If the stones would have been hidden there they could have been destroyed and I would have had to leave you buried in the snow until someone found you in the spring," Miguel yelled at Sanchez. *Sanchez knew he had screwed up but his temper got the best of him at Mike's house and the fire had gotten out of hand. He couldn't let that happen again,* he thought.

Sanchez was now standing inside the trailer that Sam called home. It was much neater than the other two. *Maybe people who are carpenters are naturally neater than bricklayers and plumbers,* thought Sanchez. As he started to move through the house, he was surprised by a cat that suddenly appeared in the doorway. As Sanchez stood looking around the room for places that may hide the gems the cat rubbed up against his leg.

He remembered having a cat when he was a child. The cat kept the mice from eating the little food they had. He remembered the feeling of the cat rubbing against his leg those many years ago. As he went to pick up the cat, his cell phone went off almost making him wet his pants.

"*Sí*,"

"I know where the stones are. You don't have to look any further. Blow up the house. I want to meet with you and Palo in a half hour at your motel room," Miguel said then hung up.

Sanchez hung up his cell phone and walked to the kitchen. He couldn't understand Miguel. One minute he yells at him for having the house catch on fire and now he wants the trailer blown up. Miguel must have a very good reason or he is starting to lose his mind. It wasn't for him to try to figure what Miguel was trying to do. He just had to follow orders. He checked the stove. Good. It was propane. He went over to the wall where the thermostat was located. He pulled off the cover. As he turned up the heat he could see a small spark jump across the contacts to engage the thermostats request for heat. Sanchez lowered the thermostat ten degrees and went into the kitchen. He turned on all four burners and blew out the flame. When the thermostat reached its new setting and sent a spark to the furnace, the propane in the house should blow the place to bits. Sanchez was ready to exit the door. He felt something on his leg. He reached down and gently picked up the cat.

Driving back to his motel room, Sanchez remembered how he loved his cat those many years ago. Sam's cat meowed in the seat next to Sanchez as he drove. Sanchez lovingly scratched it behind the ear as he heard an explosion behind him.

CHAPTER FIFTY

Miguel was the last to arrive at the motel room. Palo was rubbing his feet with cream. He wasn't used to being on his feet so much. Sanchez was watching television as Miguel entered.

"I think our mission is about over. When this Sam person goes home and finds his home destroyed, he will follow his brothers and stay at the Inn," Miguel said smiling.

"How can you be so sure?" asked Palo.

"Two now have no place to stay. I overheard the other one say there is to be a lot of snow and it would make more sense to stay at the Inn, than to ride back in the morning. I think Mike wanted to get drunk and he didn't want to drive. I will go after the stones tomorrow night. I need time to get my plan finalized. We can get away the following morning. I will drive to Pittsburgh early and we will be back in Mexico the day after tomorrow."

"Aren't you afraid of driving in the snow?" asked Sanchez.

"I have never driven in the snow but it can't be that difficult. The road to the airport in Pittsburgh is well maintained. There shouldn't be any problems," Miguel said to Sanchez.

I am going to leave tonight. I will stay with your driver and have the car loaded on the plane. The plane will be fueled and ready to go as soon as you get there," said Sanchez.

"Why are you going so soon?" Palo asked Sanchez.

"I have never driven in snow and the television weather man said there will be more than a few inches tonight," said Sanchez.

"Should I wait for you or do you want me to go back with Captain Sanchez?" asked Palo.

"Stay in case I need some help." Miguel said.

"I am scheduled to be back at work for dinner tonight. I will be at the Inn at six pm and I will stay in this room the rest of the time," Palo said.

Miguel stood looking at his two accomplices. He was close to the end of his plan to become the next great Mayan leader. When he reunites the stones with the medallion, he will place the necklace around his neck and become transformed beyond his wildest dreams. He will be the new Mayan King. He suddenly felt awake and ready to get the last phase of his plan into operation. He would shoot the three brothers with his tranquilizer gun and get each portion of the stones from them and insert them into the medallion. When they wake up, they will have really bad headaches. They will not be able to go to the police because what was stolen from them was already stolen property from the Mexican Government. It was a foolproof plan. The tranquilizer dart will knock each of them out and the gun is silent so no one in the building will know what happened. Miguel planned to take the dart out of each of the victims so no one would know what happened.

He stood by the door of the room and watched Palo rubbing his feet and staring at the television. He saw Sanchez filling his suitcase, preparing to leave. He felt sorry for these mere mortals who had no idea whose presence they were now in. He was to be King of the Mayan people. He was to be a divine leader, the greatest Mayan leader in over 2000 years. He would be invincible.

"Captain Sanchez, I will see you at the plane. Thank you for all you have done. You will be well paid upon our return to our homeland. Palo I will see you at dinner. Be ready to leave from the Inn and don't leave anything behind to trace you back to Mexico.

If something happens at the Inn, take my lead. I will make sure you are with us on the plane back to Mexico. You too will be a rich man when we return to our homeland. Good-by men," Miguel said as he left the motel and started to walk back up the hill to the Inn.

As Miguel started to walk back to the Inn, he realized he had not been able to sleep for the past few nights. Things either in his mind or in the Inn were keeping him from even an hour's rest. The ghost of his mother would race through the room at night. Lying in bed tonight, Miguel knew he would again see the ghost of his mother float through the room. He had become used to his mother invading his sleep from time to time, but these now nightly experiences were getting to him. He needed his sleep, if he was going to tranquilize the three men who had the stones. Miguel knew it was not going to be easy, but he knew the evening staff would leave by midnight and there were extra room keys secured in a cabinet in the closet behind the check-in counter.

As he looked up at the beautiful old building, he could see someone in one of the upstairs windows. It was a woman. It was his mother calling to him. Miguel was starting to lose his sense of reality. He imagined himself wearing the medallion and walking through the streets of Mexico City. All the people who saw him would bow down out of respect for his position of power. Miguel came out of his thoughts of being King as he climbed the marble stairs to the front porch of the Inn and realized he was covered with snow. Being so deep in thought about his future as King, he wasn't aware the snow was falling. He was now covered with a thin blanket of fine powdery snow. He thought what a wondrous site. He stood on the porch watching the snow fall. It didn't fall like rain. It floated in the air like little pieces of cotton. Miguel watched the snow dance in the lights that illuminated the Inn. The lights caught the snow's descent and made swirling patterns. The wind would then throw the flakes back up into the air. The sight was magical. It seemed appropriate for him to be here watching the snow fly in the sky. Some day soon he would be able to fly like the snow flakes. A breeze came toward him and the snow flew into his face. The snow was cold as it hit his skin. The snow melted quickly and chilled his face and hands. It was beautiful but the rawness of the temperature chilled him. He looked at his watch. It was now 5:30 p.m. and time for dinner. He stood on the porch and dusted the snow from his clothes. The snow was now falling much faster. *Did it always snow this fast?* He thought, as he watched it fall.

CHAPTER FIFTY-ONE

"Man, that was a good meal," Mike said as he sat on the couch looking into the roaring fire.

The other two were each sipping some twenty-year-old port.

"We need to come up with a plan for these stones," Bob said quietly as they sat in the living room. There was no one else in the room. The three of them kept their voices in hushed tones.

"Tomorrow I suggest we get a hold of our lawyer and dump them on him," Sam said.

"It pisses me off that they can kill an American citizen in another country and get away with it. We all knew Andrew. He was a great guy and a hell of a football player. He had the balls to work for his college education when he could have it given to him by his father. I keep thinking that if it was us in trouble in Cancun and Andrew knew about it, he wouldn't just walk away from us and forget he ever knew us. I don't think so. Did you guys know that it was Andrew who saved that kid from drowning in Lake Somerset the day of my graduation?" asked Mike.

"No, how come I didn't know about that?" asked Bob.

"You were probably drunk. You got drunk at everybody's graduation," Sam said.

"Very funny. How come a thing like that didn't get into the papers?" asked Bob.

"Andrew didn't want anyone to know. It was just something he did. He said he was just in the right place at the right time and left it at that. I know what happened because I saw him pull the guy out of the lake. He gave him artificial respiration. The kid started chocking and barfing out water. When Andrew was sure the kid was okay, he got up and walked away. That was it. If we needed him he would have been there for us. I don't see us just walking away from him at a time like this. I'm sure his brothers, sister, and father would like to know the truth. I know I would if I were in the same situation," said Mike.

The three of them sat for a few minutes looking at the fire and thinking.

"I think Mike is right. We need to catch the bastards that killed Andrew. We know they are in town. You know, that new waiter, I think he is from Mexico. Maybe he is here to spy on us and find out where the gems are. Now that you say that, I think someone has been hanging around outside the Inn. I'm going to have to make more of an effort to watch for strangers. Someone trashed my house and burned your place, Bob. The only one they haven't gotten yet is Sam," Mike said.

"You know I wasn't with you guys at the bar when you met Andrew. In fact, I never met Andrew when we were down there. Maybe they don't know about me," Sam said.

"Don't count on that. These guys are ruthless. If they killed someone for some gems they aren't that stupid not to know about you."

At that moment Sam's cell phone went off.

"Sam here. Hi Carol. How is everything? No, no one has called me from the police department, why? What! You got to be shitting me! You're sure? No, I know you can see from your kitchen window. When did it happen? Did it do any damage to your place? That's good. What about Cat? Oh shit. Is there anything I can do? Is it worth me coming over there with the snow falling as it is? Okay, thanks for calling. I'm all right. I hate to lose Cat but everything else is replaceable. My brothers are with me. I'll be okay. Did you see anybody around the place by any chance? I don't know. It probably was a faulty heater or something. Is there anything I could do if I came over there? Okay, thanks. I'm glad everything is good at your place. Thanks for the call. No, I'll be all right. I'm at the Inn. I'll stay here tonight and I'll get over there in the daylight after the snow stops. Thanks again for the call. Bye," Sam said and hung up.

"What the hell was that?" asked Bob.

"It didn't sound so good. What happened?" asked Mike.

"They got to me, too. My place was blown up. They made it look like there was a faulty heater. They probably filled the house with propane from the stove and somehow ignited it. There isn't anything left. The fire company is there but it blew up and there was very little fire. The snow probably helped keep any flames from spreading. I guess they know about me now. What pisses me off is that Cat was in there," said Sam.

They sat for a few minutes, each in their own now screwed up world, because of getting involved with the gems. After a little wallowing, Sam got up and went toward the door.

"I have to get a room for the night. I'll worry about my place in a day or two. Carol said there was nothing left. There was very little fire, just total destruction. I'm going to find Jon and get a room. It's not too bad outside yet. I'm going to go down to the shopping center and get some extra clothes. Can I pick up anything for you two?" asked Sam.

"The crap you buy isn't to our taste. I'll wear what I have," said Bob.

While they were in the Inn the snow had started to fall in blizzard proportions. There was at least six inches of snow with no sign of it stopping. The wind was picking up and the snow was starting to pile up in drifts.

"Mike you aren't that far away. Why don't you go home and get some rest. Just be back in the morning. We have to start fixing up the basement. Sam and I will be working on the new hallway on the third floor," Bob said.

"You want to stay with me?" asked Sam.

"I need my sleep and all your snoring isn't going to get me a good nights sleep."

Sam headed for the shopping center and Bob went to the bar.

Mike went out the front door to head home.

"It's going to be some night," Mike said to Miguel as they passed on the steps of the Inn.

"Isn't the snow fascinating?" Miguel said as he stood on the porch looking at it come down.

"I guess you're not from around here," Mike said as he continued to his truck.

CHAPTER FIFTY-TWO

"How did you enjoy your dinner, Mister Hernandos?" asked Jon.

"Dinner was delicious, and please call me Miguel."

Miguel was sitting by the fire. His experience with the snow had chilled him to the bone. There was another couple also sitting near the fire. Jon came into the room and seeing Miguel and the other couple sitting together in the room said, "Miguel I would like to introduce you to two people whom I had mentioned over the phone when you called for reservations."

"Is this the Queen of the Inn?" asked Miguel.

"It sure is. May I introduce you to Queen Susan and her husband John? You know they always stay in the Library when they are guests here. You must have impressed her when you called," Jon said.

"Queen Susan and John, I am happy to meet you," Miguel said. Miguel was now in a euphoric state of mind. He needed to wile away the next few hours. Then he would put the next phase of his plan together to get his stones. This diversion was exactly what he needed.

Susan immediately disliked the man. His black slicked hair and his pencil-thin moustache gave her the feeling this man had a life full of evil. This man was not to be trusted and she was pissed that she let the man sleep in "her" room. He was, however, a guest at the Inn and she would do her best to make his stay as enjoyable as she could.

"It is a pleasure. I hope you are enjoying your stay in 'my' room. My husband and I have stayed in a number of the other rooms in the Inn, but after you stay in the Library, all the other rooms cannot compare," Susan said.

"I agree. Jon has mentioned, in passing, that you could tell me a few of the secrets of this magnificent old home. Is that true?" Miguel asked.

"I can tell you things, but many of the tales need to be believed. Are you a believer?"

"A believer in what?" asked Miguel.

"In the spirits," Susan said.

Susan suddenly stopped and turned to Jon, "Did you smell that?" asked Susan.

At that moment all in the room experienced the aroma of roses wafting in the air.

"Roses?" asked Miguel.

"Exactly, our resident ghost makes her presence known through the fragrance of roses."

"Who is this ghost?" asked Miguel.

"Some say it is the spirit of Lizzy Zimmerman. She lived here for many years after her husband D.B. died. She may have found the house too nice to leave. Some say it could be a maid who is looking for her lost child. What kind of ghost do you think it might be?" asked Susan of Miguel.

"I do not know but I often see the ghost of my late mother. In fact she visited me in my room last night."

Miguel had never told anyone about his dreams and visits from his ghosted mother. He didn't want anyone telling him he was crazy, but here in this room with people who also see ghosts, it was as natural to talk about them as it was the weather. Miguel was opening up in a way he never expected to happen. His thoughts started to run rampant. Were these people talking to him because somehow they knew he was going to be Mayan royalty soon? Would he show these people his medallion encrusted with the stones he was going to steal back? Would he have them bow down as he told them that he was a great King?

Miguel's mind raced through these thoughts and more. He started to see the ghost of his mother again sitting on the couch next to him. He didn't want to tell these people about his mother sitting next to him. He knew they were to be trusted when talking about ghosts but he had only just met them. They may be stringing him along. At any minute they could burst out laughing and pointing their finger at the crazed man from Mexico. Miguel had to be careful how he continued this conversation. He tried to compose himself as best he could.

"What else, besides the smell of roses, tells you there is a ghost here?" asked Miguel.

"The lights blink and the electrician can never find any problem. We have watched the candles flicker from a breeze when no breeze could be explained. We have had things move. An ornament jumped off one of the Christmas trees during a conversation with my brother Denny about Lizzy. A few women claiming to be psychics have been to the house and have felt the presence of the ghost. Many signs are here for those who believe. That's why I asked you if you were a believer."

"Does any of this bother you?" asked Susan.

"Of course not," he said. "In my country there are many who feel close to the ghosts of their ancestors. We in Mexico feel that ghosts are those who have crossed over to the other world, but some come back to help the less fortunate. Other ghosts come back to comfort those still on this side of life."

"Do you ever come across any ghosts that are here because those who are still on this side of life, have done things that need to be corrected?" asked Susan.

Miguel felt as if he were slapped in the face by what she said. This remark from a total stranger knocked him back on his heels. He stood up and moved to the edge of the fire. He stretched out his hands as if trying to warm himself. This type of ghost sounds like the one that talked to him as he stood on the edge of the precipice when he put on the medallion for the first time. It was a demanding voice from the beyond. A voice that told him to do what the voice said or he would be thrown into the fire of damnation. He would rot in hell for eternity. Miguel didn't know how to answer the question.

Susan was not looking at him. She seemed to be concentrating on her knitting. Miguel looked over as the needles seem to be moving faster and faster. The needles were moving without Susan touching them. They were moving so fast they were just a blur. He watched the scarf getting longer and longer. The end of the scarf started to move across the floor toward him. He was afraid the scarf was going to move up his body and strangle him.

"Miguel," said Jon breaking Miguel from his delirium.

"Susan was only asking if you thought in Mexico, there were more people who believed in the spirits than in this country."

"Oh, I don't know a lot about your country, but I think we in Mexico are more in tune with the spirits than you are in this country."

Susan, not being the type of person who liked others deciding what she meant, asked Miguel, "Have you seen any spirits while you have been in this house?"

"I have only been here for one night and the only spirit was that of my dear departed mother."

There was a minute of utter silence when it felt as if time stood still. Then Susan looked up from her knitting and said to Miguel, "My only caution to you, Miguel, is that if the spirit of Lizzy comes to visit you, you had better do as she says. She seems to visit men only on rare occasions and when she does—well let me just say she makes a very strong impression."

Susan knew that she would apologize to Jon in the morning about what she had said to Miguel, but now she needed to have him feel a little uneasy. *I hope this man doesn't do anything while he is here to ruin the reputation of the Inn,* Susan thought.

CHAPTER FIFTY-THREE

"Damn it. I knew I should have gotten that new battery as soon as I got back from Cancun," said Mike as he got out of his truck. The snow was more than six inches deep and there was no sign of it letting up. He headed back to the Inn hoping Jon had a room. He surely didn't want to have to bunk in with Sam or Bob.

"I hope you have a room Jon. My battery is dead and I need to stay the night," Mike said as he brushed the snow off his coat.

"I have the Roof Garden available. Sam is in the Trumbauer and Bob is in the Garrett. The three of you can share the top floor."

"I thought your apartment was up there, too," Mike said.

"I've moved my apartment back by the kitchen so you can replace the wall that was in the original house."

"That's right. We are going to make another guest room on the third floor. The fire marshal said we needed a second means of egress from the third floor. The back staircase will serve that purpose."

"It will reduce the size of my apartment but an extra bedroom will improve revenue," Jon said.

"Thanks Jon. It's getting bad out there. I'll worry about my truck in the morning. Do you know if Bob and Sam went up to their rooms?" asked Mike as his cell phone went off.

"Hello, yeah Sam. Okay. I'm downstairs. My truck wouldn't start. I'll be up in a minute. Do you want me to bring up anything to drink?" asked Mike.

"Jon, I'll have three beers. Sam and Bob have something important to talk about."

Mike walked up to the third floor and knocked on the Trumbauer guest room door. He went in and found the two sitting in chairs looking out at the rapidly falling snow.

"What's so important?" Mike asked as he passed out the beers.

"Bob got a call from Penn State regarding Andrew. He was going to tell me but decided to wait to tell both of us at the same time," Sam said twisting off the beer cap and tossing it into the trashcan.

"Why did Penn State call you?" asked Mike.

"It seemed Andrew sent some papers back to the University regarding some of the things he found, namely the medallion and necklace. He also explained what was happening to him in Cancun," said Bob.

"Why did Andrew wait so long to tell the University what was happening?" asked Sam.

"Andrew wanted to write a book about his finds. The book would have kept him in good standing with his bosses at the University. He wanted to have something solid to show for his work at the Mayan site. If he started making noise about the items being stolen and sold by the local police, he would never have had a chance to complete the work he wanted to do. Andrew told the University things had gotten out of hand with the discovery of the crypt and the necklace. He was going to come back and tell them about his find of a Mayan tomb and maybe he would have a better chance of gaining credit for what he had found. It didn't quite work out that way. Andrew was killed by those crooks. He was smothered in the hospital by someone who had been stealing the artifacts he found."

"Where does that put us with these gems?" asked Mike.

"Sam and I have agreed to give them up. They have caused us nothing but trouble. We knew you would agree."

"I'm glad we are to be rid of these things," Mike said.

"There is still the problem of the guys who are after this stuff. They are here and will kill to get them. Our only advantage is that we know what they want."

"Why don't we call the local police and give the gems to them for safe keeping?" asked Mike.

"The University said we could do that but then the news media would have everyone believing that it was us who stole the gems. We could be blamed for Andrew's death. The Mexican crooks would like nothing better than having us as the fall guys for the murder. They would then get off free and clear and we would be in jail. We do look guilty having Mexican relics in Somerset. We would be out of the construction business in no time if people around here thought we had anything to do with the theft. We need to hang on to the gems until we hear from the University again. They have been in contact with the Mexican authorities. They may be sending someone up here to help us find the men who are after the gems. We need to wait," said Sam. The three sat and drank their beer as the snow continued to pile up outside.

Palo quietly moved away from the door of the Trumbauer and down the stairs to the Library. He used the key Miguel had given him and entered the room.

CHAPTER FIFTY-FOUR

Miguel called Maggie for room service. He asked her to have Palo bring him some tea.

"I want you to go up and listen in on the men that are staying on the third floor. They have something going on. I need to know what they are saying," Miguel said to Palo as he placed the tray of tea on the table. Palo quietly made his way to the Trumbauer. It didn't take long before he heard the news Bob told the other two. Now, back from listening at Sam's door, Miguel sat him down and began to question Palo.

"What did you find out?" asked Miguel.

"The University knows that Andrew was murdered. They told the men up on the third floor. The University has been in touch with the Mexican Government. The Mexican Government is going to send someone to help trap Andrew's killers. They want to help the University without telling the local police. They fear being caught with the stones, because local people will think they stole them, and maybe they were the ones who stole the stones and killed Andrew."

"That is good news. You have done a great job. You will be paid double when we get back to Mexico. I am working out a plan to get the stones and be out of here by tomorrow night. Whatever happens, you do not know me. Do you understand?

No matter what happens, you do not know me. I will get you out of this country and when we all get home to Mexico you will be a very rich man. I will need your loyalty. Can I count on you Palo?" asked Miguel.

"I will do whatever is necessary *Señor Miguel,*" Palo said and took his now empty tray down to the kitchen.

Before Palo left the room Miguel said, "That was a good job you did on that truck so that man named Mike had to stay for the night. I will not forget all you have done."

CHAPTER FIFTY-FIVE

Miguel could hear the mournful sound of the wind as it swept through the cracks of the 95-year-old mansion. Standing in his room all dressed in black, he looked out at the snow piling up against everything in its way. It was now two a.m. and the house had been quiet for the past few hours. The only sound he could hear, besides the wind and the heat circulating on and off, was the sound of his breathing. Miguel opened the back door of the Library Suite. The reason he wanted the Library was because the web site for the Inn showed it to be the only room with two means of egress. It had one door that led to the top of the main staircase. The other led out of the room toward the back staircase. He was a cautious man in most everything he did and having two ways out of his room gave him the edge he liked. Miguel was now out in the hallway and hidden by the staircase that lead to the third floor. He passed the Hillside Manor Suite. He could hear slight snoring sounds from the occupants. He proceeded down the main staircase to the lobby. The light shining in from the large windows above the landing flooded the top portion of the staircase and cast dark shadows on the lower portion. He would have to remember where the darkest places to hide would be in case he needed them for the real test tomorrow night. He went to the closet at the check-in counter where the keys were kept. This would be easier than he thought. The door was unlocked. He needed the duplicate keys for the three rooms on the third floor. He carefully opened the door. There were a number of keys hanging on hooks. Each key with a brass tag, stamped with the name of the room on it. The names on the brass tags were hard to read in the semi-darkness. Picking out the three brass keys was not going to be the quietest thing to do at two o'clock in the morning.

Miguel stood for a minute and looked at the tangled hanging keys. His eye caught a key with a paper tag on it. It seemed odd that one key would have a paper tag and all the rest shiny brass tags. He carefully picked the paper tagged key off the hook and read the label. It said "MASTER." Miguel couldn't believe his luck. Maybe it wasn't luck but special powers from the medallion, or maybe his godlike qualities were starting to come through. This paper tag with its key hanging from it made him feel like the king he was about to become.

Suddenly, as Miguel was walking toward the staircase, he felt a cool breeze pass over his face. He almost dropped the key onto the hard marble floor. *That would surely raise a stir from somewhere in the house,* he thought. The breeze turned into the smell of roses. Roses! Was Lizzy watching him? This was her house and Miguel was up to something she didn't like. Susan's words came loudly into his ears:

If you ever hear the voice of Lizzy you better do what she says.

Miguel stood and listened. All he heard was the dull sound of the wind outside and the heat coming on inside.

Miguel started up the stairs with great trepidation. Calming himself, he tried the key in his own door first. The key slid in smoothly. He turned the key and the door opened silently. It was now time to try the doors on the third floor. The first door at the top of the stairs was to the room of the one stud he had not met. He had seen the other two in the bar that night but the one called Sam was unknown to him. He thought for his dry run he would test the other two rooms. He made his way silently down the hall to the door of the Roof Garden. The key turned easily and the door opened. He entered the room. With the loudness of the snoring he could have made all the noise he wanted and not be heard. If he were to shoot the man with the dart tonight, there would be no problem. He made a mental note for tomorrow to shoot this one last. The noise he made would cover any sounds coming from the other rooms.

Listening at the door of the Garret, Miguel could hear no snoring. He carefully opened the door. He again entered and moved into the room. He could get a clean shot of the man sleeping in the bed after taking one step into the room. This could be a quick shot. As he turned to leave the room, he could hear the man pass gas. Before Miguel could get the door closed, the smell attacked his nostrils. *It would be a pleasure to shoot someone like that just to stop the air pollution,* Miguel thought as he closed the door. Miguel stopped at the door to the Trumbauer again. He listened but heard no noise from inside the room. He waited for a few seconds as he mentally turned the door knob, entered the room and shot the man in the bed.

Satisfied he could accomplish all three shots in less than three minutes, he made his way back down to the lobby and hung the key back where he had found it. He quietly ascended the stairs and returned to his room without being seen.

Being a light sleeper, Sam awoke to the sound of someone walking very quietly and slowly down the hall. Whoever it was, stopped in front of the door to the room, waited for a minute and went down the stairs to the second floor.

I wonder who that could be at this hour. At the verge of getting up and finding out who could be wandering the halls at two o'clock in the morning, Sam turned over and went back to sleep.

Miguel undressed, and before getting into bed, stared out of the window at the snow. It was still falling very quickly. The shopping center below was so covered with snow it was hard to tell where the roofs stopped and the sidewalks began. *There must be a few feet on the ground,* thought Miguel. It was good he was waiting one more day. There didn't seem to be any way he would have gotten out of the Inn at dawn tomorrow.

He lay in bed thinking of what had to be done in the morning. He had to call Captain Sanchez and tell him to wait one more day. He was sure there wouldn't be any planes flying out in the morning and maybe the entire day. He would make sure his chauffer, pilot, and Sanchez were ready for a quick departure the following morning. He also wanted to put his plan into action that would have him free of any interference from The Three Studs. Now that he knew about the call they received, he could make his plans to keep everyone in the Inn more off guard to assure his success. What he needed now was a good night's sleep. If only his mother would stay out of his life for this one night. If only Lizzy would leave him alone a little longer. He would leave the Inn and never return. Lizzy could have her house all to herself. He would not bother her ever again.

As Miguel lay in bed looking up at the light dancing off the ceiling, he saw his mother. She must have read his mind. She started to scold him for the things he had done wrong as a child. She read from a list of all the people he had killed during his lifetime. Miguel covered his eyes and ears with a pillow. His mother's voice seemed even louder. He sat up and took some of the pills his doctor had given him to let him sleep. After hearing the list read over and over again, he finally drifted off into a fitful slumber.

CHAPTER FIFTY-SIX

Miguel awoke with a start. He was soaking wet from his nightmares. In his dream he was again standing on the edge of a great chasm with eternal blackness below. He was wearing the necklace but the stones were missing from the medallion. A voice from deep in the chasm was telling him to find the stones, but he couldn't move. Heat from deep in the chasm would shoot up. Blisters formed on the skin of his bare feet. He couldn't move his feet away from the edge. An image appeared from the other side of the chasm calling to him. It sounded like his mother's voice calling him to come to her. He wanted to get away from the edge of the precipice but couldn't. He fought to move his legs. Finally, as his feet started to move over the edge of the chasm, he woke up. He lay there trying to catch his breath as his heart raced and his hands shook. He glanced at his watch. It was seven-thirty in the morning. He looked out the window to see snow still falling. The distant road that he watched the last two mornings with cars taking their drivers to work was empty of travelers. No movement could be seen from his window. The land was white, quiet, and serene. The smell of cooked bacon finally moved him into action. His stomach growled for food. This was to be the day that would change his life forever. He would have to put on the best performance of his life. He would have to convince the people in the Inn he could be trusted.

Freshly showered and wearing his Mexican leather pants, blue shirt, and leather vest, Miguel came down the stairs. He had to find Jon, sit down with him, and have a serious conversation. Miguel didn't understand the significance of the snow that had piled up during the night. No transportation would be moving until the streets and highways were plowed. No one would be going to work or school. Miguel found Jon on the phone talking to someone about the delivery of supplies needed to keep the Inn running. As soon as the phone hit the cradle it would ring again. This time it was a cancellation of a planned breakfast meeting of thirty people. The tables had been set the past evening and were ready for the group that now would not be there. Miguel decided this was not the best time to try to get Jon's undivided attention. He knew it would have to be soon if he wanted to have his plan work. Miguel could hear a man on the television reporting the blizzard that took Somerset County by surprise. Four feet of snow had fallen during the night and the state transportation workers had gone out on a wildcat strike to improve their wages. The local government was calling for a state of emergency and all non-essential employees were to stay home. All roads were closed and the National Guard was being mobilized to get emergency supplies through and rescue stranded motorists on the highways.

Miguel started for the sun room where breakfast was being served. Upon entering, he met the only other guests besides himself and The Three Studs, Susan and her husband.

"Good morning. Isn't this exciting?" asked Susan.

"I have never seen snow fall before. Does it always come down so fast and so much?" asked Miguel.

Susan laughed and said, "This is very unusual to have so much snow so quickly. A few inches, maybe a foot, but four or five feet cause's everything to shut down, even up here where they are used to snow. We are in for an interesting few days," she said.

"A few days? I have to leave for Pittsburgh tomorrow morning," Miguel said.

"You may have a problem. Nothing is moving now and if the snow doesn't stop soon you won't be going anywhere for a while."

At that moment Jon walked into the room.

"Well, folks, don't we have ourselves an interesting day ahead of us? And Susan you now have your wish of being snowed in at the Inn." Jon said.

"Isn't it wonderful!" she exclaimed.

Miguel decided this was as good a time as he was going to get to start the ball rolling on his plan. Standing up, he approached Jon.

"I need to talk with you in private," Miguel said seriously.

The two of them went into the deserted living room.

"I have something to tell you and I need for The Three Studs to be present," Miguel stated.

"My goodness, this sounds serious. Let's go up to the third floor. They are working on some renovations up there. It was lucky they stayed last night. They can get a full day's work in without any interruptions," Jon said as they climbed the stairs.

They made there way to the third floor. Two of the three were working on installing drywall.

"Where is Sam?" asked Jon.

"Down in the basement getting the trim for these walls. Why do you need Sam?" asked Mike.

"I wanted to have all of you together but this will have to do. You can fill him in on what I have to say," Miguel said.

Miguel takes out his identification and flashes it to the three of them quickly.

"I am with the State Police of Mexico. I have come up here to find the killer of a man named Andrew Kosco. The killer is a Mexican who has been stealing state antiquities from Mister Kosco for almost two years. We have been watching him for the past few months and after he killed Mister Kosco he came here to find a treasure that was supposedly taken out of Mexico by The Three Studs. Now I know that taking treasure out of Mexico is punishable by a very long jail sentence and I do not want the three of you to be punished if you were only doing a friend a favor. I'm sure you had no idea of the magnitude of the offense. My first concern is to catch the killer and I have been told to let the antiquity problem be handled by Pennsylvania State University and the Mexican Museum officials. I want you to know that the killer is here in the Inn. His name was given to me just this morning when I called back to my assistant who is now stuck in Pittsburgh."

"You mean your chauffer is a Mexican agent too?" asked Jon.

"That is correct. I was expecting to take Palo back with me to Mexico as soon as possible. This whole episode is to be kept as low key as we possibly can keep it," Miguel said.

"Palo is a murderer?" asked Jon astonished.

"Yes. He killed Mister Kosco with a pillow while Mister Kosco was recovering from a gun shot wound that Palo himself had inflicted."

"How do we know that you are who you say you are?" asked Mike.

"Let me make a cell phone call and you can ask any questions you like."

Miguel dialed his cell phone and Sanchez answers the phone.

"This is Captain Hernandos. I have someone here who needs to know if I am with the State Police of Mexico. Will you confirm who I am for him?"

Miguel hands the phone to Mike. Mike hears someone in the background speaking Spanish.

"To whom am I speaking?" asked Mike.

"This is Captain Sanchez, of the State Police Department in Mexico City. What can I do for you?"

"I wanted to make sure this man that is with me is really from the State Police Department," Mike said.

"Miguel Hernandos has been on the police force for over twenty years. Does that answer your question? I am real busy. Is there anything else I can do for you?" asked Sanchez.

"No, that is all. Thank you," Mike said and handed the phone back to Miguel. Miguel spoke to Sanchez, "We plan to leave tomorrow morning for the airport. There is a lot of snow and the plane can't leave until then. See you as soon as possible with our prisoner."

"Are there any other questions?" asked Miguel

Everyone shook their heads.

"What do you want us to do?" asked Mike.

"I want to take Palo as quickly and as quietly as possible. I do not want to upset any of the other guests and I want to find a safe place to keep him until I can take him out of here tomorrow. Do you think we will be able to get out of here tomorrow?" asked Miguel.

"The storm is pretty localized. We have the most snowfall in the County. There is only four inches in Pittsburgh, so we should be cleared out by tomorrow morning for you to get to the interstate and out to Pittsburgh. That Hummer you bought yesterday will help you get through to Pittsburgh," said Jon.

"That is good news. I know that Palo is staying at a nearby motel. Has he made it to work yet?" asked Miguel.

"I saw him coming in as I was going into the breakfast room. He was to be here to serve the breakfast meeting that now has been cancelled. He is probably in the kitchen. How do you want to handle this?" asked Jon.

"Is there a place in the house that we can keep him until tomorrow morning?" asked Miguel.

"There are rooms in the basement that can be used if you tie him up securely," Jon said.

"I may need your help," Miguel said to Mike and Bob.

Mike and Bob were so ecstatic that they were not going to be taken back to a Mexican jail, they would have been happy to carry Palo back to Pittsburgh for the flight to Mexico.

"What do you want us to do?" they asked.

"Come with me and help me tie him up. We can keep him in

the basement until we can leave. Jon you will need to show us the way. Oh, by the way do you have the jewels in case someone asks me at the Police Station?" asked Miguel as his heart started to race.

Mike pulled out the chain from around his neck. There on the end of the chain was a single large ruby. Bob pulled his necklace from under his shirt. A very large emerald was suspended from the chain. Miguel couldn't take his eyes from the stones. He couldn't believe he was so close to two of the twelve stones he so eagerly sought.

"Are you ready to go?" asked Bob as he put the necklace back under his shirt.

Climbing out of his daze, Miguel nodded his head. The four of them left the third floor and proceeded down the back staircase to the kitchen.

"Follow my lead," Miguel said.

Miguel, for some reason only his warped mind could explain, had a set of handcuffs with him. As the four made their way down the final set of stairs to the kitchen, Miguel started talking.

"This is an interesting old house and I'm glad you took me on the tour, Jon. Did the people who worked here ever use the front staircase for any reason or were they relegated to the rear set?"

By the time Miguel finished asking the question he was standing next to Palo, who was walking toward the rear door.

"Grab him!" demanded Miguel.

Mike and Bob easily grabbed Palos arms and wrapped them behind him. Miguel applied the handcuffs. Miguel started talking to Palo in Spanish

"Be quiet. I need to do this so we can get away tomorrow morning. You will be going with me. Now don't make a fuss. I need your cooperation. Do you understand?" Miguel said.

Palo nodded and didn't resist as the handcuffs were wrapped around his wrists.

"Jon, if you will lead the way to the basement."

"What did you say to him?" asked Bob.

"I read him his rights and told him he would be going back to Mexico for trial," Miguel said.

Jon took them through the vestibule. He turned right, then through a curtained door down to the basement. The stairs were wide enough for two men to escort Palo, one on each side. At the bottom of the stairs the hallway went both right and left. Bare-bulbed lights hung from the twelve-foot ceilings illuminating each doorway they passed. The basement had not changed from the days it was first built. The walls were the original plaster and paint. At the end of the hall directly under the existing living room was a space of equal size used by the Zimmerman family for their amusement room. There were also rooms for the laundry, storage, and a boiler room with an area built for coal storage. The old coal furnace had been replaced with a new gas-fired furnace. The modern furnace looked inadequate to provide enough heat for the big house. When the house was built a sleeping room had been provided for a person who was responsible to keep the coal furnace running. A room that had no windows and was deemed the best place to keep Palo until the following morning. The bare bulb that now provided light to the room reflected off a pile of old doors and shutters that once graced the house. A sturdy wooden chair was found for Palo to sit on for his duration at the Inn.

"There is a back staircase through the kitchen but it was too narrow for escorting our prisoner," Jon said after they had Palo safely settled and tied to the chair.

"I will take the first watch. If I can find a way to secure Palo so we all could go about our business, I will let you know, but for now, I will stand watch over him. Jon, if you could come back in a few hours to give me a ten minute break I would appreciate it. If you can't, maybe one of the gentlemen could do that for me."

Bob and Mike jumped at the chance to do whatever they could for Miguel. It seemed much better than going to jail.

The three men seemed to be congratulating themselves as they made their way back up to the first floor. After Jon, Mike, and Bob were gone Miguel started talking to Palo in Spanish.

"First, does anyone on the staff speak Spanish?" asked Miguel.

"I have not heard anyone speak it, and when I have said something in Spanish I have not gotten any reaction, so I don't think anyone speaks it," said Palo.

"That's good. We can speak freely. I had to do what I did. I couldn't figure out another way to get these gringo's into my good graces. I was sure they thought I was the one the police would be looking for. I had to use you. I'm sorry my friend, but it had to be done."

Palo sat still absorbing all that had just happened. He was most amazed that Miguel called him his friend. It made him feel he was contributing to Miguel's success. He knew Miguel rewarded loyalty very well. He knew if he followed directions, when they returned to Mexico, he would be well taken care of. He had seen others who were in the good graces of Miguel. Each of them never had to worry again about where their next meal would be coming from or if their families would have enough food or clothing. Loyalty to Miguel would make him a wealthy man and his family would be very happy for the rest of their lives. Palo was happy to be tied up in a chair in a dismal basement in Somerset, Pennsylvania, to make all that happen.

"What do you want me to do?" asked Palo.

"Just sit tight and tomorrow we will be on our way to the airport and back home. I have to make these people believe you are the killer and they have nothing to fear. I want them to trust me. It will make it easier for me to get the stones that I am looking for," Miguel told him.

Miguel stopped talking when he heard someone approaching. Two women passed the doorway carrying dirty sheets and towels, heading toward the laundry room. Jon must have told them there were two men in the basement and they were not to be disturbed. The two women glanced into the room but continued to walk with their laundry toward the other end of the basement.

"Ladies may I have a word with you?" Miguel said in Spanish loud enough for the women to hear.

Neither lady came back.

"Why did you do that?" asked Palo.

"Just checking to see if they knew any Spanish," Miguel said smiling.

"Is there anything I can get you?" asked Miguel.

Palo was happy to just sit and wait for tomorrow. His wrists were a little sore from the handcuffs but he didn't mind. It would only be until tomorrow morning. He had eaten breakfast and he didn't have to go to the bathroom, so he was comfortable for the next few hours.

"I am fine. I can sit here for the next few hours before I will need to pee. I have no needs at this time, Thank you, Mister Hernandos," replied Palo.

"Listen I have a plan and I may need your help. I am going to get the stones tonight. I am going to try to make it easier by getting as many of them drunk as I can this evening. Before I go to bed I will come down and release you. After I release you stay in the basement and listen. If you hear anything that sounds like I may be in need of help, come up the stairs and assist me. I would rather you stay here until morning. I don't want anyone to get suspicious. After we leave the building we will be on our way back to Mexico."

"Isn't there going to be someone here with me tonight?" asked Palo.

"I will tell them I will be on duty. I plan on having a party tonight and get all of them drunk. That way we will have less trouble with them. Don't worry. I have everything under control."

Miguel heard some noise out in the hall. The two women

were walking by talking and carrying freshly laundered towels. They seemed to have become accustomed to the two men sharing their basement with them.

"I hear someone else coming. Quiet," Miguel said.

CHAPTER FIFTY-SEVEN

"Man we have a lot of shit to tell you. Where have you been?" asked Mike and Bob.

"I was down in the basement getting the trim for the walls you guys were building. I found a door that we could use. It's a six panel and it's still in great condition. I could move the hinges and have it up by the end of the day," Sam said dropping the trim on the floor.

Bob and Mike started telling Sam all that had happened. They told about the capture of Palo and his incarceration in the basement.

"Where the hell were you when we took Palo to the basement?" asked Mike.

"I must have been taking a pee or I was in the back corner of the basement pulling some of the trim that had been left near the outside stairwell. The place was full of snow. We can't afford to have that stuff warp. That trim cost us a pretty penny. If it's ruined it comes out of our pocket. I know you guys don't always think of that but that's the difference between profit and loss on a job," Sam preached.

"Hey, we know that stuff. This was more important than a little trim. We're in the middle of catching Andrew's killer. Miguel had us hold down Palo so he could handcuff him. This could bring us more business if the people in Somerset know we are heroes," said Mike.

"Slow down, I don't understand. How did you know Palo was the killer, and are you sure Miguel is with the Mexican authorities?" asked Sam.

"Yeah, He got a phone call from Mexico and he showed us his credentials," said Bob.

"What did the credentials say," asked Sam.

"Hell if I know. I can't read Spanish. I had to take French in high school. You were the Spanish major. You should have been there. You could have asked all these questions," Mike said.

"Okay that's part of the answer but how did he know Palo was the killer?

"Miguel got a phone call from Mexico. He has an agent waiting in Pittsburgh to take them back to Mexico tomorrow."

"So Miguel is in the basement with Palo and they are going to leave in the morning to go back to Mexico. Is that right?" asked Sam.

"That's it. We are supposed to keep the gems until someone from the University gets in contact with us."

"Why don't the Mexican authorities want them sent back with their man?" asked Sam.

"They don't want to draw a lot of attention to them. They don't want it to become an international incident," Mike said, proud as a peacock.

"Did Miguel ask to see the stones?" asked Sam.

"Yeah," said Mike.

"What did he say when he saw them?" Sam asked.

"He was a little gaga over them. In fact he was a lot gaga," Mike said.

"Well, I guess we are off the hook. All we have to do is hold on to the stones until the University calls us. The best thing for us to do is finish this hallway and get some lunch," Sam said, knowing it was close to noon and Mike and Bob would be starving by now.

CHAPTER FIFTY-EIGHT

"I have come to give you a break," Mike said as he entered the room.

"Thank you, Michael. May I treat you to lunch?" Miguel asked.

"I just finished eating and it's Mike. No one calls me Michael, not since my mother died."

"It seems such a funny tradition in America. Most men get a Christian name when they are born and yet they end up with a nickname. Does anyone ever call your brother Robert?" Miguel asked.

"I guess not. It just seems to be the thing to do. I never thought about it," Mike said.

"This other brother I seem to keep missing. Sam, is that short for Samuel?" Miguel asked.

Before Mike could answer, there was loud stomping directly above them. The noise surprised the two men.

"I had better go up and see what all that noise is about," said Mike.

Mike was back in a minute, "Daniel just accepted a delivery of food that came in the front door. The back door was snowed in."

"The trucks are finally getting through?" asked Miguel.

"Just barely. The man has a business down the street and it took him an hour to go three blocks. Things are getting better but the state snow plow workers are still on strike. The city workers are pushing snow in town, but the roads still aren't very good yet. Roads should be passable if the state guys get their act together and get back to plowing the Turnpike. It should be okay for you to get out in the morning," Mike told him.

"That reminds me. I would like to have a party tonight and all the food and drinks will be on me. Your brothers, the other guests, and those that work here will have anything they want on me. How does that sound?" asked Miguel.

"That's great, I sure could use some cheering up, and the rest of the people, I'm sure, would be more than happy to eat and drink for free. Thanks Miguel. I'll watch this guy for a while. You can go up and tell the others. What time are we going to start the party?" asked Mike.

"How about we start at five o'clock with drinks, and we will keep going for as long as we can stand up?" said Miguel smiling.

"That sounds good to me, now take a break. I'll stay as long as you need."

Miguel went up the stairs with a big smile on his face. *This is going to be easy,* thought Miguel.

CHAPTER FIFTY-NINE

"I think we should finish up for the day. We need to get ready for the party tonight," Mike said.

"You haven't done much today, you might as well leave," Bob said disgustedly.

"What do you mean? I've been carrying my load," Mike said.

"Listen, each of you has been looking at your watches since you found out you are going to get free food and drink. You are like two kids waiting for Christmas. No your acting more like you do the day before deer season starts. You just walk around looking at your watch and dreaming about that big buck you're going to shoot. Why don't both of you get cleaned up and get to the bar to make sure you don't miss one minute of the free drinks. I'll finish cleaning up the sawdust and get the trucks cleaned off for tomorrow. Mike, I'll clean off your truck so you can get to that dead battery. You can't charge it with all the snow on it."

"You would do that for me? Thanks Sam. When are you going to get down to the party?" asked Bob.

"I'll get there in plenty of time for dinner. Don't worry about that. Now you two get out of here and let me get some work done."

The two of them were out of the room in a flash. Sam grabbed the broom and swept the floor. The third floor renovation would be complete after a little painting. That could be started in the morning.

Finishing the cleaning, the thoughts running through Sam's mind became clear. No one seemed to be at all concerned about the true identity of Palo. Jon told Sam that Palo came out of nowhere one day and applied for a job. He said Palo had papers to prove he was in the country legally, but had limited time to talk with Palo to find out much about his background. He knew how to wait on tables and he was very industrious. Jon was pleased with his work and that's about all there was to the story about Palo.

This story told by Miguel was starting to bother Sam. After getting the tools to the basement, Sam stopped to see what Palo was doing. He sat tied in his chair. The housekeeper was watching him from a distance. Her diminutive frame would be no threat if Palo would get free. She smiled as Sam entered the room.

"Why don't you take a break for a few minutes? I'll watch him while I put these tools away. The housekeeper left quickly. Sam continued to put the tools into the large wooden box labeled Three Studs Construction Company. Sam finished storing everything away and secured the top with a large padlock.

"There. Everything has been put away for the day," Sam said out loud. "Tell me Palo, I hear you killed someone in Mexico. What made you kill a man who probably wasn't going to live anyway?"

Palo didn't answer. He sat tied in his chair with his chin on his chest.

"You know my brothers and I were friends of Andrew. He was a good man and didn't deserve to die that way. He saved a man's life out in the lake that you can see from the back of the house. He didn't think it was anything. Saving lives was what you should want to do if you had the chance. But you, Palo, you take lives. You know I talked to Jon and he thought you were a very good worker and was totally surprised that you were a murderer. Sam slowly walked toward the chair Palo was sitting in. Walking closer, Sam's still gloved hand picked up a piece of hundred-year-old pipe that was lying on the floor.

Standing at full height with pipe in hand and toe to toe with Palo, Sam said, "What the hell made you kill an innocent man. He was trying to help your country find its past. He was trying to make a difference in this world. Why did you kill him? Sam yelled as the pipe came down and smashed against the ground.

"Palo screamed in fright, "I didn't," he stammered in Spanish and started to cry.

The housekeeper reentered the room, slightly shaken by the noise she heard as she came down the back stairs.

"What happened?" she asked meekly.

"I'm sorry. I got pissed. He is the man who killed Andrew Kosco."

"Nobody told me he was a killer. I was told he was a man being taken back to Mexico but not that he was a killer. Oh my goodness," she said, as she put her hands to her mouth in aghast.

"Don't tell anyone what I just said. This is to be kept a secret."

"I won't tell anyone. I can watch him for a while now. The night manager, Sophie, is working this evening and Jon said she could take the next hour."

Sam was sure there was more to this Palo thing than Miguel was saying. *There needs to be a little more investigation,* Sam thought.

CHAPTER SIXTY

"Man, the bar looks better tonight than last night," Mike said as he sat on a barstool looking at the décor.

"That's because tonight you are not paying," said Bob.

"I think I heard you two at each other last night," said the bartender.

"We have been doing this for as long as we have been allowed to drink at a bar. I don't know why, it just happens. We don't do this any other time," Mike said.

"You do it all the time. You never give me a minute's peace," Bob replied.

"That's not true. We work well together."

"As long as I'm doing all the heavy work you don't seem to mind."

The bantering continued as Jon came out from the kitchen carrying hot hors d'oeuvres.

"Where is Sam?" asked Jon.

"Sam is Sam. Had to finish cleaning up the third floor and needed to get a few other things done. Supposed to be here for dinner." Mike said as he drank some more beer.

Miguel came into the room.

"Here is our host. Let's have a toast to Miguel. Have a safe trip back to Mexico and thank you," Bob said.

"Bob you better thank him now before you drink yourself under the table," Mike interjected.

Jon walked back into the kitchen as Sam appeared down the back stairway.

"Jon I need to talk with you," Sam whispered.

Jon and Sam moved back into the storage area in the rear of the kitchen.

"Do you know where Palo was staying?"

"At the motel on the other side of the parking lot, why?" asked Jon.

"For some reason I don't trust Miguel. There is something about him that gets to me.

I'm going to go over there and get whatever possessions Palo has left in his room. He will want to take them with him when he leaves tomorrow anyway. No one seems to have thought of it. Let's keep this just between the two of us for now. I'm going to slip out through the basement so no one sees me. I don't want to have to answer any questions. Okay?" Sam said quietly.

"Be careful, it's dark out there and the snow is pretty deep."

Sam slipped down the backstairs to the basement. Palo was being watched by Sophie.

"How's the party going? I hate to miss a party," she asked.

"How did they get you to do the happy hour?" asked Sam.

"Jon caught me when I came in and I said sure, before I knew there was going to be a party and that I was included. Where are you going?" asked Sophie.

"I need to get some of my gear in order and some of the snow off the truck so I'll be ready in the morning."

"How are the roads?" asked Sam.

"Everything is getting back to normal. It took them all day. The snow plowers went back to work. They hated to lose the money since we haven't had that much snow this year. We should be fine by morning. What's with this guy anyway?" Sophie asked as she directed her head toward Palo, "I thought he was doing a good job upstairs."

"He's wanted in Mexico and Miguel is supposed to take him back tomorrow. All you have to do is watch that he doesn't try to gnaw through his ropes and get away, said Sam, putting on gloves and heading toward the back door.

Sam went directly out and down to the motel. The trip didn't take as long as expected. A plow from the shopping center had pushed a path that led to the motel.

"Charles, how the hell are you?" asked Sam entering the lobby of the motel and stomping off the snow.

"Not bad. What brings you here in all this snow?" Charles asked.

"We have a problem at the Inn," Sam said and proceeded to tell Charles about Palo and Miguel.

"You know I can't let you in the room without a warrant or policeman present."

"Charles, you know I have police training and I'm part of the Auxiliary Police Force. Sam flashed the brass Auxiliary Police Force badge.

"I can't."

"Sure you can. Let's just go down to the room and you can open the door and I can look in. I won't touch anything. We just need to look."

Sam and Charles finally agreed on a quick look around the room. If there is anything that looks suspicious, the local police would be called in the morning. The two walked down the covered walkway.

"Here it is, room three."

As they got to room three, Sam whispered to Charles, "I hear something."

"It sounds like a cat inside," Charles said.

"Open the door," shouted Sam.

Sam could tell by the meowing that it could be Cat. The door opened a crack and Cat squeezed out the opening and jumped into Sam's arms.

"Cat, I thought you were dead. How did you get here?"

Sam told Charles of the explosion at the trailer and the expected loss of Cat.

"The only way Cat could have gotten here is if Palo had something to do with it," Sam said excitedly.

Charles opened the door and they walked in. A suitcase was lying on the floor full of clothes and ready for a quick departure. The room was clean and nothing was out of place.

"We need to see what is in the suitcase," Sam said, petting Cat.

Charles moved the suitcase on to the bed, opened it, and looked inside. Clothes were neatly stacked. A shaving kit and wallet were the only non-clothing items in the suitcase. Sam put Cat down and opened the wallet. Staring back was a picture of Palo in a uniform. Across from the picture was a badge.

"What does it say?" asked Charles.

Sam read the Spanish words. It said Mexican Police Cancun, Quintana Roo District

"It says Palo is a policeman and the guy at the Inn is telling us Palo is the one who killed someone in Mexico. That seems a little fishy," said Sam, petting Cat.

"I should call the police now," Charles exclaimed.

"Don't do that. We don't know anything for sure. Let's wait. I would take the clothes and keep them in the office if I were you. How long was the room paid for?" asked Sam.

"It's up tomorrow, but I wonder where the other guy is? I really can't take anything out of the room if the guest is paid up. I have to leave everything as is until tomorrow morning."

"What do you mean the other guy?" Sam asked.

"There was another guy staying here. I think his name was Sanchez. I only saw him when they checked in and again yesterday."

"What time did you see him?" asked Sam.

"I just happened to see him leave yesterday just before it started to snow. He shook hands with Palo and drove off. It seemed from his actions that he was leaving town before the snow started. I don't see any other clothes here so I guess he really did leave. Maybe we should call the police," Charles said nervously.

"Like you said, they have paid for the night. The only thing that is suspicious is having Cat in the room. We don't know the circumstances behind that so there is no reason to get the police involved. With the mess from the snow they are probably up to their eyeballs anyway. Let's just keep the lid on this whole thing until tomorrow. Can we just move the suitcase under the bed? Is that against the law?" asked Sam.

"I don't know. I've never had anything like this happen to me before."

"Let's just, between you and me, push it under the bed. I'll not tell anyone that we were ever in the room, except I want my cat," Sam said.

Sam pushed Cat into a shopping bag Charles found in the office and walked back to the Inn. Sam cleaned the snow from Mike's truck as quickly as possible. Cat didn't move from inside the shopping bag as Sam brushed the snow off the truck. Entering the rear door, Sam could hear the party in full swing. Rather than go into the bar, Sam went up the back stairs, carrying Cat in the shopping bag.

Sam lay on the bed petting Cat. *This whole deal with Palo seemed to smell*, Sam thought. Miguel is here for the gems. Sam was sure of that. Miguel was more than likely the one who killed Andrew. Sam knew it wasn't Palo. He was being used by Miguel but why? Mike's house was trashed by someone looking for the gems. Bob's place was burned to the ground for the same reason. Palo was working when my place was destroyed. There was someone else involved. It must be that Sanchez guy Charles mentioned that was sharing the room with Palo. But why is Sanchez not here to help get the gems? Maybe Sanchez isn't part of the plan. Then there must be someone else. Palo is a policeman. Sam remembered something almost forgotten. Sam went to the jacket hanging in the closet. In the inside pocket was a little present that was lifted from Palo's suitcase without Charles knowing it. Sam removed Palo's wallet. In the wallet was the badge from the province of Quintana Roo, in the town of Cancun. The photo identification didn't give any more information except that Palo was a patrolman and a Captain Sanchez was the person running the police station. There was a phone number. Just for the hell of it, Sam called the number.

"Buenos dais may I speak to Captain Sanchez?" Sam asked in fluent Spanish

"Captain Sanchez is not here. May someone else help you?"

"May I speak to Palo please?"

"I'm sorry they are both out of the country at an important meeting. Can I be of assistance?" asked the person on the other end of the phone.

"It is not that important. I was told they knew Miguel Hernandos. I was wondering if they knew where he is. I have to send a package to him and I can't locate him."

"You are a friend of Mister Hernandos?" asked the person on the phone.

"Yes, I have some gems he was interested in."

There was silence on the other end of the phone.

"I can't help you. Call back in a few days," Roberto hung up the phone and wondered who would have gems to sell to Mister Hernandos. He didn't want any part of Hernandos and his dealings. He wanted to be a good cop and good cops didn't take bribes. It took a lot for Roberto not to get in line to get some of the easy money given out by Miguel Hernandos. He loved his job and he didn't want to jeopardize it for a few pesos. Roberto was getting hungry and had to pee. He got up from the desk and immediately forgot about the phone call.

Sam lay back down on the bed with Cat. *What was that all about?* Sam thought, while scratching Cat. There is some guy named Captain Sanchez who has been helping Miguel. Palo was put on the inside as a waiter and Sanchez has been on the outside. Sanchez was staying with Palo. Sam noticed that both beds had been slept in but, Sanchez isn't around any longer. Did Miguel kill him and dump the body somewhere? Sam thought about that for a minute. Sanchez must have left Somerset before the snow. He had to be the one who did all the damage to Bob's place and mine. Sam had one more call to make.

"Hey, Janet, this is Sam. How's my favorite cousin? Don and the kids okay? Great, oh you heard about my place blowing up? It was a faulty heater. I was glad I was at work when it happened. I'm staying at the Inn at Somerset for a while. We are renovating parts of it and it makes the commute to work real short. Thanks. The reason I called has to do with something for me. I will be able to tell you about in a few days. I promise it's going to be a great story. We can do it over lunch at the Inn. I was hoping you could help me. I need to find out if a man with the last name of Sanchez rented a car at the Pittsburgh airport probably two or three days ago, and if he has returned it yet. You can do that? Great, Yeah, I'll buy lunch and one glass of wine. I can't have you driving that police cruiser around with liquor on your breath. When can you let me know? Oh really? I'll wait."

Sam stayed on the phone while Cousin Janet's fingers danced over the computer keyboard. In less than a minute she was back.

"Captain Manuel Sanchez rented a Jeep from Quick Rent three days ago and he is to return it tonight. He used cash. Is there anything else you need?" asked Janet.

"That's it for now. I will call you tomorrow evening and fill you in on all the details."

"How are your brothers doing? Janet asked.

"The two shits are doing okay. They are now in Jon's new bar here at the Inn getting drunk on someone else's tab. You can't ask for anything better than that. Yeah, I'm going to join them in a few minutes. Someone has to get the work done. Talk with you tomorrow. Thanks again."

That fills in another piece of the puzzle. It's always good to have relatives on the police force, especially one that runs the computer with access to everything in the police files, thought Sam, lying on the bed petting Cat again.

CHAPTER SIXTY-ONE

"This is a great party. We even have a pianist" yelled Bob over the laughing of the crowd.

"I should have done this for the staff a long time ago," Jon said. Sally got a real surprise when she stopped in to see if we needed any help because of the snow. She managed to make it to her swimming class and dropped in to say good- bye to Queen Susan, who is going home tomorrow. She was also curious about having enough help for the party of twenty-five we were supposed to have tonight for dinner. She didn't know that the party was cancelled this morning. We have plenty to drink, lots of food and Helen's apple strudel," Jon said.

"I just tried one of the new martini's with *Quintessential* Gin. That stuff is good. I think I'll have another," Bob said as he walked back to the bar.

"Ladies and gentlemen, I have to take my turn down in the basement watching our prisoner. I will be back for dinner in two hours. Please drink up, and Jon, bring out more of that Beluga Caviar. I hope you have some more," Miguel said.

"If you have the money, we will find more caviar." Jon replied.

Miguel reached in his pocket and pulled out a roll of hundred dollar bills. He passed twenty to Jon and added, "If that isn't enough, please let me know. I will be back in two hours. I hope someone will come down and relieve me so I may spend some time at dinner with everyone," Miguel said.

"We could bring him up here for a few hours. He may be hungry and lonely being down there with the night manager," replied the bartender. Everyone laughed. Miguel waved and went to relieve her in the basement.

Sam had finally figured out who was who. Miguel was the rich guy who was stealing Andrew's treasures. Sanchez was helping get the treasures to Miguel. Palo worked for Sanchez and got the shitty end of the stick. Sam sensed that something was not quiet "right" about Miguel. From what his brothers had said, the guy thought he was a Mexican official. He knew how to take a situation by the horns and he knew how to control a crowd. Everyone was now thinking he was a great guy. Sam had different ideas. This guy wants the gems and will do anything to get them. He has killed once that I know of and killing seems to come easy after the first time. The classes for being an auxiliary cop at the police academy made that very clear to Sam. Sam would have to stay sharp tonight and listen to what is said about Miguel.

"Hey, Sam, you just missed Miguel. He went down to take over so Sophie could come up for a drink. Why don't you go downstairs and meet him?" said Bob.

"That's okay, the nights still young. I'm sure I will be spending some time with Miguel.

CHAPTER SIXTY-TWO

"I'm here. The party can start. May I have one of those "Q" martinis?" Sophie asked as she entered the bar.

"I will take care of the phone if it rings. No one should be coming in, with this kind of weather," Sophie said as she took a sip of her drink.

Jon seemed to sense there was something wrong. He had been in the bar for almost an hour and the phone hadn't rung. *I hope the lines aren't down from all the snow,* he thought. Jon slipped into the office. He picked up the phone. There was no dial tone. He reached into the top drawer of the desk for his cell phone. That was working, thank goodness, he thought. You never know if you will need it in case of an emergency.

The party was going well and he had to get more of that wonderful Beluga caviar. Thank goodness there was a ten ounce container in the refrigerator. It had been ordered for the dinner that had to be cancelled. *At least it won't go to waste,* Jon thought smiling as he felt the wad of hundred dollar bills in his pocket.

CHAPTER SIXTY-THREE

Miguel went to the basement to talk with Palo. On his last trip down there he found the junction box for the incoming telephone lines. On this trip he brought a knife and cut the lines. He wanted all the advantage he could. He had taken some food and a bottle of beer for Palo. He made sure there was no one downstairs and released the handcuffs on Palo.

"Here is something to eat and I brought you a beer. Are you doing okay?" he asked in Spanish.

"I am fine but that woman who was here. She wanted to know everything about me. She never knew a murderer before and she wanted to know how I became a murderer. I was about ready to become a murderer. If you had not come down here, I may have somehow gotten loose and killed her. Women in Mexico speak only when spoken to. These American women have too many freedoms," ranted Palo.

"I understand but it won't be for long. We are getting close to our goal. All those people upstairs love me and they think I am a wonderful person. They don't know that I just cut the phone lines. If no one can call in we won't be bothered by interruptions. It will keep the police and the University from interfering for the rest of the night. Tomorrow we will get out of here and be gone from this country. You will be rich and I will have achieved my goal of being the next great Mayan King. The stones, after they are placed into the medallion, will allow me to do whatever I want. No one will be able to touch me. I will be invincible," ranted Miguel.

Palo didn't understand most of what Miguel was saying nor did he care. All he wanted was to be back home and living a life that would make him his own king with the money he was going to get from Miguel. Miguel could be whatever he wanted to be. If he wanted to be the King of the Mayans, so be it. Palo just wanted to be king of his own little family. Palo was quiet as he ate and drank. He just wanted the night to be over so he could be on his way back home.

Sam wanted to keep an eye on whatever Miguel did. The back stairs to the basement went through the kitchen. Sam silently slipped down the stairs. The trip was made easier because Sam could hear Palo speaking loudly in Spanish to Miguel. Sam heard all the conversation and especially enjoyed Miguel's ranting about becoming a Mayan King. It was more difficult getting back up the back stairs now that Palo had stopped ranting about Sophie. Sam slowly placed each foot in front of the other hoping there weren't any squeaky steps. If there were, Sam would have to move fast. With luck and the practice of walking on the outer most edges of the steps, Sam made it back to the kitchen with the last piece of information needed to take down Miguel.

CHAPTER SIXTY-FOUR

The bar was jumping. Susan, her husband, the Studs, Jon, Sophie, the housekeepers, and waitress's along with the kitchen staff were whooping it up all on Miguel's money.

"Ladies and gentlemen I have another special treat for you this evening, as if we haven't had enough," the bartender said from behind the bar.

"Our friend, James, has left a bottle of *Anejo Tequilla* for us to partake. This beautiful bottle was hand blown in Murano, Italy, especially for this sipping tequila. Everyone gets to sample this fine liquid gold. Please do not push. There is enough for everyone to taste but not enough for everyone to drink."

The crowd was past the point of no return. It was a drinking frenzy. With everything free, it was a chance not to pass up. There were plenty of delicious salted peanuts and deli delights from Susan's cousins that helped everyone drink more than they normally would. The hangover tomorrow would be from a free drunk. It couldn't get any better than that.

"I think I need to get Miguel. This crowd needs to eat something. The dining room is ready and the waitress's and cooks are ready to serve," said Jon to the crowd, but no one moved.

"There will be all the drinks you want served with dinner, so please find a seat in the dining room," Jon said.

Miguel could hear people moving from the bar to the dining room. He had to get upstairs to see what was going on. He didn't want anybody too sober. He had work to do tonight and he wanted all the advantage he could get. Miguel heard footsteps coming down to the basement.

"Miguel, you need to get upstairs with your guests. I will take over," said Jon.

Miguel moved quickly to get back to the party and make sure everyone had as much wine as he could pour in them. He entered the dining room as all were just seated.

"Where is Sam?" Miguel asked.

"Sam was just here a minute ago," said Bob.

"Sam went down to the basement so Jon could come up. He needed to be part of the dinner. The staff needs an extra hand and all the other hands are a little too tipsy," Mike said.

Sam went down the back stairs and entered the room where Jon was watching Palo. Jon started to leave and Sam followed him to the stairs.

"Jon, before I forget, what rooms do you have open on the second floor? Before you answer I would prefer the Lakeview," Sam said.

"Is there something wrong with the third floor?" asked Jon.

"No. I just need the room for something tonight. I'll explain everything tomorrow. I promise."

"The key I gave you is a master. It will fit in any of the rooms. Don't know what you are up to, but we can talk in the morning," Jon said.

CHAPTER SIXTY-FIVE

Everyone had eaten and drank their fill. Many of the people were going to drive home tonight and thought they better be on their way. As Miguel and Jon bid those that were going home adieu, Sam relegated Mike to watch Palo while Sam moved a few clothes from the third floor to the Lakeview room on the second floor. Leaving the room on the third floor, Sam locked the door and padded to the second floor without being seen. The necklace was made a stratagem for Sam's plan to be successful.

The guest host Miguel, was saying good-bye at the front door to the last of the party guests. Now there were just seven people left in the house and one prisoner tied up in the basement.

"Now that we have reduced the number, why don't we bring Palo up here while we all have one last drink for the night?" Miguel said.

"One last fire. We also will be leaving tomorrow, "Susan said.

Jon stoked the fire and added the last log from the receptacle now just full of splinters and bark. The flames soon crept along the sides of the new fuel and gave a warm glow to the room.

"A little Port would be about all I could handle. Is anyone else interested?" Jon asked as he came into the room. No one answered. All seemed to be occupied with their own thoughts.

Mike, Bob, Susan, her husband, and Jon sat by the fire as Miguel and Palo came into the room.

"Where is Sam?" Miguel asked.

"Sam went to bed. Not much of a drinker. Sam likes to get to bed early," Bob told Miguel.

"Too bad I was looking forward to a little conversation. It seemed every time I anticipated meeting the last of the Three Studs, something interrupted the experience."

"You didn't miss much," Mike said as he stared into the fire.

"Well tomorrow Jon, your Inn will be back to normal. Palo and I will be gone and you will just have The Three Studs to grace the mansion, and all this trouble for some stolen jewels. The two stones that I have seen were very beautiful, but surely not worth taking a human life," Miguel said as Jon poured everyone a drink of twenty-year old Port.

"Do you think I could see those jewels again before I leave to go back to my country?" asked Miguel.

"I can show you the emerald," said Bob reaching into his shirt to remove the necklace.

"Here is the ruby," Mike remarked.

Miguel started to get weak in the knees at seeing the gems that would turn him into a Mayan King. He asked, "May I hold them?"

They each handed Miguel their necklace. Miguel could almost feel the power of the stones as he looked at them. As Miguel stood looking at the stones, a slight breeze could be felt flowing through the room.

"Do you smell that?" asked Susan.

"Roses," Jon said as he took another sip of his Port.

"She is here. I don't think she likes those jewels," Susan said.

As she said that, the lights dimmed.

"Now I know she doesn't like them," Susan repeated.

Miguel held a necklace in each hand. His heart was racing. Thoughts of his future raced through his head. He wanted those stones in his medallion now. He wasn't sure he could wait for the next few hours until he would steal them and put them in the medallion where they rightfully belonged.

An image of his mother appeared and raced through the room dashing toward the roaring fire. Miguel almost jumped forward to stop the ghost as it disappeared into the now roaring fire. Just then a loud snap from a piece of burning wood echoed through the room like a gun shot. Miguel jumped.

"It's only the fire," Susan said. "Did you see something Miguel?" she asked mystically.

"No, no it was nothing," he said as beads of perspiration formed on his forehead.

"I think it is getting late and I think Lizzy has had enough for tonight. See everyone in the morning," Susan said as she got up to leave the room with her husband following close behind.

"We have a full day tomorrow too. The third floor walls will need to be painted and we will be starting on the basement renovations. I need to get some shut eye too," said Mike.

"I hope you will keep those necklaces safe while you sleep," said Miguel.

"We keep them on the night stand right next to us. Sam does the same so that when the University calls, we will be ready," Mike said as he finished his Port and headed for the door.

"I'll take the first two hours with Palo tonight as I promised," said Jon.

"No, I think I'll tie him up and keep him in my room. I'll tie a bell on him so if I fall asleep I'll hear him," laughed Miguel.

Everyone was too tired to disagree. The blazing fire died as fast as it had come to life. They each took a last look at the embers in the fireplace and headed to their rooms.

CHAPTER SIXTY-SIX

The hours moved slowly as Miguel sat looking out of the window. The snow was piled up along the paths that had been plowed for the people using the shopping center. The lights bounced off the snow piles making weird shapes in the snow banks. Miguel's watch now read two a.m. Palo was asleep in the bed with one of his hands still locked in the handcuffs. Miguel had changed into his black shirt and slacks. He wore his black walking shoes on his trial run the night before. Tonight he had double knotted the laces to be sure he wouldn't have an accidental trip along the way. He made the walk up to the third floor fifty times in his mind. He could wait no longer. He was tempted to wear the medallion and insert the stones as he took them from the three, but thought he had better keep to his original plan. He was too superstitious to change plans now. His biggest concern was Sam. Was he big or small? Did he sleep lightly or, like his brothers fart and snore all night? Listening at Sam's door last night, neither farting nor snoring seemed to fit. Miguel didn't think of asking Palo what the third stud looked like and now he didn't want to take the time to quiz him about the third stud. Sam would have to be dealt with first just in case he was a light sleeper. He would be out of the way and wouldn't have the chance to ruin the gathering of the other two stones.

Bob and Mike had consumed so much alcohol that Miguel didn't think anything would wake either of them. Miguel had cleaned the dart gun three times. The gun had come in handy a number of times in the past when he had to convince a few people that they should pay up their debts. After the debtors awoke from the dart's drug, they were glad they were still alive and paid up all their debts very quickly. Killing someone wasn't a problem with Miguel. He had done it dozens of times, but after he killed someone that owed him a lot of money, he realized he couldn't collect what was owed him. The dart gun had proven itself very useful over and over again. Tonight it would prove itself one more time and it would be the most important time of all. The drug would wear off in six to eight hours and the studs wouldn't have any idea what happened. After Miguel put the necklace together he would retrieve the darts. In the morning he and Palo would be gone. The Three Studs won't be able to go to the police to report the theft because they were told to wait for the University officials to get involved. By the time the University officials got to Somerset, Miguel would be back in Mexico and he would be King of the Mayans. He would be their God. He would be able to do whatever he wanted. He would laugh at the world and all of its petty problems. He would be omnipotent.

Miguel finally got himself back under control. It was time. He slowly opened the front door of his room. Easily making his way down the front stairs to the check-in counter, he opened the closet where the keys were kept. The key with the paper tag was exactly where he had left it the night before. First he would go into the room of Sam, then Bob and lastly Mike. He would go back to his room, insert the stones and become all he could imagine and more. He started walking up the grand staircase. He was worried that he had not seen the ghost of his mother since he watched her disappear into the fire. Holding that thought in the back of his mind, he took the master key that was clutched in his hand and climbed the stairs to the third floor.

CHAPTER SIXTY-SEVEN

Sitting in the corner of the Trumbauer, Sam waited covered in a dark blanket. Someone could be heard coming up the stairs. The key was quietly slipped into the lock. The door opened and a man dressed all in black came into the room. Standing at the doorway with the light shining through the window, Sam could see Miguel holding some sort of gun. Miguel saw the necklace lying on the nightstand. He quickly and silently picked it up, pointed his gun at the sleeping body and fired. A silent thump went through the covers and Miguel was gone. Sam waited a few seconds until steps could be heard going down the hall. Sam removed the blanket and crawled out from the dark corner of the room. Slightly shaken by the experience, Sam quietly walked to the door. Hearing Miguel enter the Roof Garden, Sam went to the bed. The pillows were made up to look as if there was someone sleeping. A dart was sticking through the blanket and into one of the pillows. Sam pulled the dart out and headed for the door.

CHAPTER SIXTY-EIGHT

Miguel made it past the first Stud. *Sam wasn't that big of a challenge after all,* he thought. Mike was next. The room reeked from Mike's passing gas. Miguel again found a necklace lying on the night stand. The stone was shimmering in the light that was cascading through the unshaded window. Miguel was momentarily drawn to the stone. He wanted to pick it up and hold it. He quickly regained his senses and returned to his plan. A fresh dart was shot through the covers into sleeping Mike. Miguel retraced his steps out of the room. His body was tingling. He had two of the three pieces he needed. *Only one Stud to go,* he thought as he closed the door and exited the room.

CHAPTER SIXTY-NINE

That son of a bitch came into my room and tried to knock me out. He will stop at nothing to get the gems. Sam's first thought was for the safety of Mike and Bob, but Sam knew that Miguel was only shooting knockout darts. The last necklace Miguel needed was in Bob's room and that was his next stop among the third floor rooms.

Sam checked on Cat, who was sleeping in the closet, then took the newly created hall to the back staircase and silently made it to the second floor. The rear stairs were for the servants use when the house was built and came down to the servant's bedroom area on the second floor. Sam opened the door leading to the main bedrooms and passed the rear door to the Library. There was heavy snoring coming from the room. *Palo,* Sam thought. Sam had to take care of Palo just in case Miguel came back and wanted to use him to help with his escape.

Reentering the Lakeview, Sam picked up a few items especially left by the door. Back to the Library, and with the master key Jon had given each of the Studs to make their work easier, Sam slipped into the Library. Palo was lying in bed with only one hand cuffed. As Sam got close to the bed, Palo sat up and said in Spanish, "What are you doing in this room? I will shout and you will be caught. I'm not afraid of you anymore. Miguel is my friend and he will take me back to Mexico where he will become King of the Mayans"

Palo didn't have a chance to say another word. Sam clobbered him across the back of the head with a one-hundred year old brick. *That's for my bricklaying brother,* thought Sam, who knew there would be a good use for the old brick. Palo went down on the bed and was out cold. That should hold him for a few hours, thought Sam as Palo's other hand was re-cuffed around the bed post.

A noise from the third floor had Sam scurrying back to the Lakeview.

CHAPTER SEVENTY

The snoring from Bob's room was worse than the night before. All the booze made him noisier than ever. Miguel used his key and entered. The necklace with the ruby was lying on the nightstand. Miguel first shot the dart into the comatose body. The snoring stopped for a second and then started again. Miguel picked up the necklace and exited the room. Miguel couldn't believe it. He had all three necklaces. He had to stand in the hallway and look at his success. The ruby and emerald were huge. The diamonds were not all there. There was one diamond missing. There were only nine diamonds. Where could the other one be? Had it fallen out in the room? In the hallway?

Maybe it wasn't there from the trip from Mexico. Miguel wasn't sure what this would mean. Would the medallion give him the powers with one of the stones missing? Miguel searched the hallway.

He opened the door to Sam's room to see if the diamond had fallen on the floor. There was no sign of the stone. He would have to go with what he had and hope for the best. He could get a replacement stone the same size and brilliance, but would the medallion have the same power? Miguel was starting to get concerned. Maybe all of this was going to be in vain. He couldn't think that way. This all couldn't be in vain. The feeling he had when he put on the medallion when it didn't have the stones, was amazing. With the stones it would be miraculous. Miguel had to get the stones back into the medallion as soon as possible.

CHAPTER SEVENTY-ONE

Sam could hear Miguel's footsteps from the third floor. Would he shoot darts into Jon, Susan, and her husband?" Sam had to end this before someone else became involved in this fiasco. The last phase of Sam's plan had to be put into effect now. Sam had dressed the part and was ready at the bottom of the steps from the third floor. Sam started to moan as Miguel started down the third floor stairs, "Miguel, what have you done?" Sam said in Spanish.

Miguel stopped midway down the stairs.

"Who is that? Is that you Momma?" Miguel asked in a whisper.

"Miguel what have you done. You have committed a mortal sin. You are not God. You have sinned in the eyes of God. There is a reason you do not have all the jewels. It is against God's will. There is no other God but our heavenly father," Saying this in a ghost-like voice. Sam walked out into the hallway and pointed at Miguel.

"I will come after you. You will have to pay for your actions."

Sam ducked back into the Lakeview and waited for Miguel to come through the door. A four foot length of pipe was ready as soon as he came in. Miguel went into a frenzy. He had to get the stones into the medallion. With the stones back where they belong, even the ghost of his mother couldn't bother him

He quickly made his way down the stairs from the third floor and entered the Library. He went immediately to the desk. The tools were waiting for the delicate operation of removing the stones from the necklaces and reinserting them into the medallion. His hands stopped shaking as he started his delicate work. First the Ruby was reunited. The medallion seemed to glow when the stone was inserted. Next came the emerald. Miguel could feel warmth coming from the medallion ... One by one the diamonds was inserted back to their original locations. With each diamond, the medallion seemed to become lighter. It seemed to levitate itself off of the table. Nine of the ten diamonds were now in place. Miguel sat and looked at his handy work, afraid to touch it. The medallion was beyond belief. Miguel could see that the stones started to produce a glow of their own. Before he put on the necklace, he went to release Palo. He wanted him to see what was going to happen when he put the necklace on. He wanted someone to bow down to him as he became the King of the Mayans. Miguel shook Palo.

"Palo wake up. I want you to witness my greatness. Palo get up. What is wrong with you?"

Miguel couldn't wake Palo. He turned Palo on his side and was surprised to see Palo's handcuff attached to the bedpost. He released the handcuffs. It was then he noticed a huge knot on the side of Palo's head. He could see that Palo was breathing but he couldn't be awakened. He couldn't wait. He would have to do this without him. He took the medallion and the chain and walked to the front door. He wanted to be out in the hallway when the power hit him. The other people in the Mansion would surely be able to see the difference that was to overcome him when he wore the necklace. Standing in the hall, he placed the necklace over his head. He could feel a tingle but then he heard that voice again coming from the stairs to the third floor.

"Miguel, you have failed. Without the last jewel the necklace has no power. You will never become King without that stone," the voice said.

Miguel could see something appear in a white flowing gown. The ghost of his mother had come back.

"Momma is that you? Have you come back to punish me, or do you want to see your son become King of the Mayans? All I want is to be King of our People. You told me so many times that I was to be King. Now is the time," Miguel said in Spanish.

Sam ran back up the stairs to the third floor and down the back stairs to the kitchen.

Sam had waited in the Lakeview for Miguel to come into the room. When he didn't Sam moved into the hallway. Sam heard Miguel trying to wake Palo. He wanted him to see the change that would take place when he put on the necklace. Sam moved up to the third floor to again frighten Miguel into pursuit. Then Sam would clobber him with the piece of pipe. After trying to entice Miguel up the stairs didn't work, Sam went back up the stairs to the third floor and ran quickly to the back staircase and down to the kitchen.

Entering the foyer from the kitchen, Sam walked amongst shadows up the grand staircase to the first landing. Miguel was standing just outside the door to the Library.

"Miguel," Sam said in Spanish.

"Is that you Mother. Where are you? Do you now see me as the King of the Mayans? Can you see the magical Medallion I am wearing? I am now King of our people!" Miguel said as his voice became louder with each sentence he muttered.

"I am not your Mother. I am Lizzy Zimmerman the owner of this house."

Miguel turned white. The power of the necklace was temporarily forgotten.

"You have cursed this house with your craving for power. My husband, may he rest in peace, had power and what did it do for him? It killed him. He ended up with no heirs to his fortune. Power kills. Miguel, you were told to listen if you heard my voice. Now I command you to come to me. Come to me now!" the haunting voice chanted.

"Come to me now!" chanted Sam holding the four-foot piece of pipe ready for a final blow.

Miguel, with the necklace around his neck, walked to the railing that overlooked the foyer. He looked down to the landing. The ghost moved into the light streaming in through the windows above the landing. He could see the most beautiful ghostly woman in a long flowing gown standing on the landing. In her raised hand was the last of the ten diamonds. He had no choice but to do as he was instructed. Lizzy must have known all along what his plan was. She wanted Miguel to come to her for the final stone to make him the King of the Mayans. He walked to the railing and looked at the woman in the flowing gown.

A voice, deep in Miguel's brain, spoke to him, "Do as she says." It was the voice he had heard standing at the edge of the precipice in his dream the first time he put the necklace on. Miguel knew it was the power of the necklace wanting to capture the last missing diamond. The necklace would give him dominion over all forces real or ghostly. The necklace was pulling him as if a magnet was pulling him toward the beautiful Lizzy and the diamond. There was only one thing for Miguel to do and that was to follow the necklace and become the ruler of his people. Miguel climbed over the railing and stood on the edge of the second floor. He followed the bidding of the necklace and leapt toward the beautiful woman. Miguel knew he could fly. The medallion would give him the power to soar through the air and snatch the last gem from the fingers of the beautiful Lizzy. As Miguel jumped off the balcony, Sam stood in horror as Miguel's leap was well short of its mark. He landed on the hard white marble floor below. Miguel's broken body quickly joined his long lost Mayan ancestors.

Sam could hear Jon coming from the back of the house shouting something about what was that noise. As she made her way down the last few steps, Jon came around the corner.

"What in the world! Samantha, what are you doing walking around at this time of the night?" Jon said. She pointed toward the front door. Jon walked to the vestibule and saw the body of Miguel lying on the cold marble foyer. The white marble now streaked with Miguel's blood.

CHAPTER SEVENTY-TWO

The police had arrived. The coroner's office had taken away Miguel's body. The women who cleaned the Inn had managed to get all the blood stains off the marble. Jon was going to need a new carpet, but other than that there were no indications anything happened. Palo had finally regained consciousness and was in the custody of the Somerset Police awaiting extradition to Mexico. The Pittsburgh police had Captain Sanchez and the chauffer in custody. The only piece of the crime yet to be dealt with was the Mayan necklace and medallion.

The Three Studs were sitting on the sun porch having breakfast and waiting for the officials to arrive from Pennsylvania State University.

"The pastry chef has outdone herself with her special cinnamon rolls this morning," Mike said as Jon entered the sun porch.

Jon sat down across from Samantha who had finally recovered from her ordeal with Miguel.

"Now that most of the police are gone, what the hell happened last night, Sam?" asked Jon.

"Well it's kind of a long story. I'm sure I'm going to have to tell this one a few times so I might as well start with you. My two dear brothers met Andrew in a bar in Cancun and after a few too many, decided they would get involved with Andrew's scheme of smuggling the gems from a Mayan medallion out of the country."

"It wasn't like that," interrupted Mike.

"We were doing a friend a favor, that's all. We didn't steal anything. We just got the stones back into the states for a friend," Bob added.

"As I was saying, these two idiots got in the middle of an antiquities theft. Being the stupid sister that I am, I was sucked into this mess. I replaced junk jewelry stones with these real ones. What they didn't know at the time was they were followed back to the hotel in Cancun. The only saving grace was that the thieves didn't know I was the third stud. They assumed I was a guy. I used my knowledge of Spanish to help me from getting drugged by Miguel's stun gun last night."

"I don't understand how they didn't know you were with them," asked Jon.

"I didn't go to the bar and when they were being watched on the beach, I was shopping. I guess they found out there was a third Stud but they still didn't know I was their sister."

"Hell, you have never acted like a sister before. We didn't think you would start now. You used to beat the crap out of us when we were growing up," Bob added.

"You're both wimps. Anyway, I got my first clue something was screwy when I was in the basement and the three of you helped Miguel capture Palo. I heard Miguel ask Palo if anyone in the house spoke Spanish. Since I had been conveniently missing they didn't know that I could. Miguel wasn't telling Palo his rights when you were in the kitchen, he was telling him to be quiet and he would explain later. When I heard that, I wanted to be in hearing distance whenever those two were together. I soon knew Miguel's plan and I knew he was the murderer."

"Why didn't you tell us? We could have called the police" asked Mike.

"We were the ones who had the stolen jewels and we knew Andrew. We would have been the ones in jail. I had to find a way to get Miguel to admit he was the one who did the killing. I wanted to play on his superstition about the ghost of his mother and the stuff he believed about becoming the next Mayan King. I had a tape recorder set up to provide evidence that he was the killer. I didn't expect him to do a header off the second floor. He put that necklace on and he thought it would let him fly. He was out of his mind after he heard all that Lizzy stuff."

"That was a very pretty white gown you were wearing last night," said Jon with a smile.

"When was this? The only stuff I see you wear is overalls and steel toed work shoes. Is there really a lady under that baseball hat?" asked Mike with a grin.

"Oh shut up. You have some painting to do upstairs and take your brother with you. I think I'm going to change the name of this company to The Two Idiots and Their Keeper."

Printed in the United States
205910BV00001B/199-216/P

9 781596 636569